The Appalachian Trail Murder Mysteries

TRACKED TO KILL

TRACKED TO KILL

BY

A.B. GIBSON

delaPomme.com

Thank you to Brianna Maguire, my trusted editor and friend.

To Scott

PART I

Chapter 1

The curious salad of letters and symbols was the only message to populate an old email address. Anyone else might have dismissed it as spam, but to Alain de la Pomme the encrypted gobbledygook from his former special ops colleague was easily decoded:

Lots of chatter in dark places. Your old friend Le Mauvais is back in New York. Want in?

The note didn't specify an urgent action or requirement to call back. There was no need. Major M was an expert at pushing other people's buttons, and Alain liked nothing more than following a fresh scent down a trail. Secret messages, secured lines, and chasing villains had always intoxicated him, and this time it only took one whiff - and it came with the bonus of unfinished business.

Le Mauvais. It was a French newspaper that dubbed the notorious assassin-for-hire with his infamous name. Due to his signature execution-style technique of snapping the necks of his targets and his knack for eluding detection, he became as well-known as his celebrity victims. He never left clues, and his anonymity made his apprehension impossible.

After three frustrating years, Alain's team finally caught a break. In a small hotel in Thonon-les-Bains, France, Alain set up a sting to catch an American real estate mogul and a Russian diplomat in an illegal transaction. It was meant to be routine, but matters got complicated when they discovered Le Mauvais had gotten to the American before the meeting began. Propped up in one of the hotel's famous therapeutic baths, the mogul's head dangled from its broken cervical vertebrae.

Though Alain never captured Le Mauvais, hidden cameras he installed in the corridors to photograph the meeting that never took place captured his face. Alain distributed physical copies of the snapshot to branches of law enforcement everywhere, and the digital version went as viral as was possible in those early days of social media. The photo was blurry and revealed few distinctive features, but it was apparently enough to send the assassin underground. While Alain was given the credit for putting an end to the brutal three-year rampage, he considered his inability to capture Le Mauvais a career failure. Ironically, instead of the photo aiding in his apprehension, because of it, Alain lost him forever.

Alain opened a secret compartment in his desk and retrieved the secured phone. He knew the number by heart.

In no time, the two friends fell into a comfortable conversational rhythm. They pretended to catch up on their careers over the eighteen months since Alain left, though the charade was unnecessary. Each had followed the other's career in detail. Soon the chitchat turned to bragging how their current positions provided such personal satisfaction. Boasting led to good-natured ribbing. While Major M praised Alain for how his GeoFibre Charitable Foundation outreach initiatives touched thousands of lives around the world, he kidded him for selling out as a corporate poohbah and for de la Pommes being in the news all the time.

"Not bad for an old guy," joked Major M.

"Hold on. I hope you notice I never let them photograph me.

We agreed Will would be the face of the company. But look at you, the number two bigwig at Interpol, in the shiny new global complex in Singapore."

"Yeah, not bad, huh? We've got a revised mission to boost cybersecurity and counter cybercrime, and we hope it will burnish our reputation."

"Yeah, yeah, blah blah. I can't lie that I was surprised you didn't get the top job."

"What makes you think they didn't offer?"

They both knew it wasn't a social call, and Alain was eager to get to the point. "Le Mauvais has been on my mind lately. Truth be told, I never stopped thinking about him. You said he resurfaced, so fill me in. I'm all ears."

Major M began with a confession. His suggestion that Le Mauvais was back in New York was not true. He used the exaggeration to attract Alain's attention, and referring to him as Alain's old friend was an affectionate jab. Nemesis was more like it.

"So, if he's not in New York, is he still in Thailand," asked Alain.

Thonon-les-Bains was a relatively small town popular with tourists on the French side of Lac Léman, and while the local authorities promised a quick apprehension, a massive coalition of law enforcement agencies bolstered with unlimited resources stepped in and quickly found dots to connect. Suspicious wire transfers and airline manifests led them to Thailand, where they believed he went to hide. Their theory was confirmed when a local operative in Bangkok positively identified him departing a bus from Chiang Mai. Le Mauvais picked up on the awkward eye contact, and he quickly disappeared into a crowd. Though he was never seen again, Major M insisted he couldn't have left the country undetected.

"Believe me, if he somehow managed to escape, it would

have been next to impossible to re-enter another country without triggering an alert at its passport control."

"I'm not following," said Alain. They both were speaking their native French, so he knew it wasn't an error in translation. "If he's still in Thailand, why are we talking about him?"

"It seems he trained a surrogate to do his dirty work. That's who is in New York."

"What makes you think it's a surrogate?"

"Do you remember that Danish journalist found dead in New York a few months ago? She was about to reveal a widespread election tampering scheme by a foreign government."

"Of course. Didn't she die from some strange liver disease?"

"Not exactly." Major M quoted from her obituary. "'She died in her sleep after losing a battle with an aggressive cancer, a battle she'd kept even from her family.'"

Alain smiled, but found no joy in hearing the variation of a line he wrote years ago to explain another of Le Mauvais' high-profile executions. "So by 'not exactly,' you mean, not at all."

"The technique was identical," continued Major M. "We flew in the same coroner from Rome who examined Le Mauvais' other victims. I even joined them personally. We're dealing with someone every bit as sinister as Le Mauvais, and whoever he is, he needs to be put out of business. And I can't do it without you. Can we borrow you for a couple of months?"

Alain's face brightened at the unexpected validation. He had to face facts. As fulfilling as it was to run the GeoFibre Foundation side-by-side with his nephew William, much of the bragging with Major M was a lie. While he wasn't entirely miserable, he wasn't exactly happy. Sometimes he felt that leaving espionage drained the lifeblood from his core. He knew his former agency would take him back any time, but the invitation from Major M was what he needed to make his move. He didn't have to think long.

"If I reassign my duties at the Foundation and tie up a few

other loose ends, I could start in a month," said Alain. "I'll work from my apartment in the West Village. I want to spend more time there anyway."

Major M was agreeable. The timeframe would allow his team to give Alain's place a sweep and install some new electronics. In the meantime, he'd reinstate Alain's high-level security clearance and get him new credentials.

"No offense, but will I be working for, um, Interpol?" Anyone in the business knew that any glamour associated with a job at Interpol did not exist outside the world of spy movies.

"Ha ha. I hope all your celebrity and wealth hasn't made you such a snob that you can't be impressed with how things have changed. Listen, my business card says Interpol, but as you might imagine, I have, shall we say, other responsibilities."

Major M explained how Interpol's public-facing makeover was his idea. So was putting himself at number two. His new position allowed him to bury the super-secret elite group he had run for a decade deep inside the organization and let him essentially hide in plain sight. Extraordinary new backdoor funding came willingly from the American, British, and European intelligence services, who were all too eager for a way to collaborate on selective and sensitive missions leaving no traces of involvement by their own spy organizations. The dazzling advanced intelligence-gathering technology their pooled resources made possible was available to them all.

"I'm not sure why I'm blustering on. I've heard your setup at GeoFibre rivals ours."

"Oh, it's pretty slick. But those deep investments were necessary to make because of our work with the Pentagon. Besides, it comes in handy for our own tracking operations."

Major M coughed. "Yeah, and for other things, if my sources are correct."

"Bah, rumors!" Alain laughed.

Though he wouldn't officially start for another month, Alain was hungry to get up to speed, and he was exhilarated when Major M offered to link him to their current intel on the new assassin right away. In a few days, Alain would be up and running and know as much as they did. In the meantime, he began to outline his letter of resignation. There were plenty of competent people at the Foundation to carry on his work, and Alain considered they may be glad to be rid of William François de la Pomme's meddling uncle.

He knew his nephew would be deeply disappointed, but Alain convinced himself that they'd figure out ways to spend as much time together as possible, even in his new role. Still, he was conflicted about how to best break the news. Will was temporarily away from the office on a several month-long holiday hiking the Appalachian Trail, and it would be another few months before he would return to the company. He hated to make such a drastic move without telling him, but he made a promise not to distract him during the hike. Instead, he set about making lists and determining how he could both take on the new job and make a graceful exit from his corporate responsibilities.

Chapter 2

Rather than scale back and postpone the implementation of new programs during Will's five- to six-month absence, the GeoFibre Foundation Board agreed to do the opposite. Their initiatives were too crucial to put on hold, and prior to Will's departure, they brought on more employees to ramp up progress.

Alain was gratified their mission continued to draw so many talented young people. He loved the new generation's openness and creativity and the lack of bias and judgement in their approach to problem-solving. Their eagerness to help tackle the world's greatest challenges was a bonus. Most of all, he loved their energy - envied it - if he was being truthful. Though he'd always looked and acted younger than his actual years, in recent months Alain was beginning to feel his age. Not that it held him back from anything. Since leaving his post with the agency, he'd been plenty busy at GeoFibre, or so he told anyone who asked. Busy was the right term. But for Alain, a life centered around a desk, meetings, and receptions was hardly what he considered active.

Compared to the thrill of his new adventure, tidying up his responsibilities at the Foundation seemed mundane. Most of his responsibilities were high-level, which naturally senior staff would absorb or manage. He would encourage some of the new people to fill in for him at the social events. After a careful perusal of his calendar, Alain was confident that transferring his work load to others would be easy and he could start working with Major M earlier than he'd originally suggested. Things would change again, and he could pick up the slack later. He wasn't going to be away permanently, after all - just long enough to take care of this one project.

His primary worry was that leaving the day-to-day work would disappoint Will. From the beginning Will often gave credit for the company's success to his collaboration with Alain. He called their secret weapon "intergenerational magic," and the popularity of this message was so compelling to audiences everywhere, a publisher begged the twosome to write a book together. The bestseller launched a series of speaking engagements, and Alain hoped a full schedule of new bookings would provide enough of a mechanism to keep them together.

Jumping back into his old work could pull them apart and was the one thing that made him nervous about accepting Major M's mission. He reached for the dog-eared file he kept in the same drawer as the phone he used to call Major M. The envelope on top contained the famous photo, an enlarged version he kept from the start. Somehow, it looked blurrier than the last time he examined it, and he wondered how much of his confidence in what Le Mauvais looked like was overstated. It occurred to him that nothing much in the file would be of value in tracking and bringing in the new killer.

Two hours later Major M called him back. "Knowing you, I can assume you're already arranging your move to New York. But listen, while we were talking earlier, my team picked up another tidbit, and I wanted to pass it along before you started buying your season theater tickets."

"You're right. I am making plans. In fact, I've figured out a way to start earlier. I was going to leave in two weeks. Are you telling me your assassin is no longer in New York?"

"I'm afraid so. We can't explain it, but everything suggests he's headed for the Appalachian Trail of all places. I doubt it's for a vacation. Some politician or celebrity must be getting back to nature, or whatever people do out there, and we are working double time to find out who it might be. Anyway, I'll let you know as soon as we find out."

Alain searched for words.

"Alain? Are you there?"

"Yes."

"What's wrong?"

"Nothing, but um, actually I'm having second thoughts."

"What! You're not backing out? I need you."

"No. I'm starting today."

Chapter 3

Will had almost reached the top of a rise when the signal from his watch caught him off guard. The shock to his wrist was gentle but powerful, and the message from the pulsing vibration sequence that followed was unmistakable. *Plan B.*

The implication filled him with dread. Still, he found it hard to suppress a smile. He was proud of his team's work and knew they would enjoy learning their ingenious warning system functioned so well, though its activation meant their boss was in peril. The guys in his lab had rigorously tested the device under many types of cloud cover and at varying altitudes, so receiving the warning on an overcast night atop a peak on the Appalachian Trail was a welcome validation.

In a few days, William François Chillon de la Pomme planned to pass through Harpers Ferry, West Virginia, the midpoint in his planned hike of the twenty-one-hundred-mile Appalachian Trail from Maine to Georgia. He could have hiked faster, but he had been taking his time and savoring each mile, because there was no telling when he would have the luxury of taking off five or six months at a time again. Now, all this would change.

The alert rattled him, but thanks to all the practice sessions with the guys in the lab, he didn't panic. The alert instructed him to abort his hike, and the vibration sequence indicated he had twelve hours to meet a rescue team at one of the established rendezvous locations. He tapped an icon to send a confirmation, then sat on a fallen tree trunk to follow through on the next step in the protocol.

To the casual observer his watch could be mistaken for a top-of-the-line Garmin Epix trail watch, the ones with elaborate GPS functions and high-resolution touchscreens. The Epix gave its users a top-class signal and Garmin its stellar reputation by linking two satellite systems. But this was no off-the-shelf product. While the engineers in his lab in Montreux, Switzerland left the exterior of the watch intact, they did an extensive overhaul of the guts. Adding the third satellite system for the alert feature was one way they customized it - and the most vital.

Until then he preferred to navigate with the map he kept in his back pocket. The feel of paper in his hands lent authenticity to his trek, and he had folded, refolded and sat on it so many times over the past two months it was falling apart.

"Sorry, old friend," he said as he slipped the map in a plastic Ziplock bag. "I need to retire you now. Those are the orders." He turned his attention to the watch. In seconds he brought up an enhanced map of the trail detailing the escape route to the rendezvous point associated with his location. After swiping and fiddling with some settings, he took the next step.

He unzipped the lower front pocket of his backpack, and his fingers went right to the USB jump drive. It looked ordinary enough, but if it fell into the wrong hands or anyone got nosey, thanks to his engineers, the thief would only find playlists and a few audiobooks. Like his watch, the jump drive was far from ordinary. He pinched the ends and twisted it apart, revealing a cavity and its real function: a pillbox. He stared at the contents and gulped. They would simply have to figure out how to reduce the capsule's size. In the meantime, he swallowed both and washed them down with an extra-long swig from his canteen.

The night would be moonless, and any attempt to find his way out at that hour would be foolish. Another twenty minutes of hiking would get him to the shelter where he originally planned to set up camp. He could leave at daybreak and still have a couple hours to spare.

Voices ahead triggered a rush of paranoia that someone had witnessed his recent actions. Taking a pill and looking at a watch were hardly incriminating acts, but he tensed anyway, until he recognized the guy and his girlfriend from earlier in the day when they were hiking in the opposite direction. The fanny packs gave them away as day hikers, but it was the multiple rings in his nose that made the boyfriend's face hard to forget. Being friendly to other hikers was an important part of trail culture, and as they passed, he acknowledged the couple with a polite nod. They were engaged in a spirited conversation, but the boyfriend attempted to smile back. It was the end of a beautiful afternoon, and Will assumed the couple was heading back to their car like dozens of other people who hike down and back small sections of the trail in a single day.

He had just put the worry behind when, suddenly, a new voice startled him. "What's up, Red Rover?" This time the hiker belonging to the voice appeared from behind.

"Just livin' the dream!" Will called after him. "What about you?"

Unlike the couple, this guy didn't reply. He sped up and within seconds was over the rise. Other than the couple, Will didn't recall seeing any other hikers on the trail that day, and he wondered why so many seemed to appear at once. As most people hiked the trail northbound, Will elected to head south for the privacy it afforded. Any hikers he would encounter, he'd meet head on, leaving less of a chance that anyone could sneak up on him from behind. So it was surprising this guy had managed to. Hikers tended to be friendly like the couple, and while the stranger's lack of congeniality at first struck him as odd, he guessed the guy hadn't heard him.

Will caught his face long enough to know he'd never seen him before. They were both about the same height and sported beards, which were scarcely distinctive. Practically every guy let his facial hair grow on the trail. The hiker had a pile of unwashed blonde hair and bluish circles under his eyes, but something else was unnerving. He didn't remember meeting the guy before, and he wondered how this hiker knew he went by Red Rover?

In his short life, Will achieved celebrity status twice: first, as a teenage model in Milan, with his ubiquitous face in magazine spreads and on billboards, and later as a high-tech superstar who frequently guest starred on television talk shows and moved from deep within magazines to their front pages. When *People* and *Time* put him on their covers, it was impossible to deny his star power. Not to mention the surprising traction the bestselling novel he'd written with his uncle was gaining.

While the publicity was good for business, he feared if someone recognized him on the trail and the news spread, it would ruin the ethos of his hike. Maintaining his anonymity was the one aspect about his super-organized adventure he had not worked out in advance, and he guessed it would only be a question of time before someone pegged him.

It turned out not to be a problem. What's known among hikers as trail magic took care of him on the second night. He had been keeping to himself near his tent when hikers sharing the same campsite invited him to join them at their campfire. He found it awkward not to accept. After a little friendly small talk, Daddy Longlegs introduced himself and his friend, Strider. The woman seated on the stump next to him called herself

Twisted Sister, and when she asked his name, Will became tongue-tied.

Her question reminded him of the last television interview before he left. The notoriously crazy talk show host introduced him by mangling his full name. Then she pretended to be flummoxed about which one of his names to call him, and she milked the studio audience for laughs when she asked them to decide for her. William or Fransoys? She deliberately mispronounced his second name again to live giggles, amped up by an aggressive laugh track.

Will smiled politely and with a rehearsed response explained that he understood how some might find so many names complicated. His first name was William, a contribution by his American mother, and François, his second name, came from his Swiss father. His American friends called him William, or Will, and his European friends called him François.

He always ended his explanation with a practiced chuckle. "So, take your pick. I answer to either!"

One of the compelling attractions of a long hike was the opportunity to live in the present, which meant starting with a blank slate and a new identity. One's past private life was unimportant to serious hikers, and they seldom used their real names. It was fun, since for most it was the first chance to choose their own.

There were plenty of names to pull from the animal kingdom and nature – like White Owl and Bobcat – but often trail names came from unexpected sources. Sometimes an outstanding trait, or quirk, or even an event might inspire a hiker to bestow a trail name for another. That explained names like Klutz and Einstein.

"I'm embarrassed," Will stammered. "I don't have a name." It was a true conundrum, since he'd been born with a mouthful.

Twisted Sister had been staring since he joined them, and it made him uneasy. "What do you mean? Of course, you have a name!" she said.

When she slid over for a better look, he instinctively stared at the ground and covered his face. She pulled his hand away and lifted his head by the chin, exposing him to the firelight and the other campers. He gulped and braced himself for the big reveal.

"You are...you're...let me think. I know it." She spent a few moments studying him, before she made her big announcement for all to hear. "You're Red Rover!"

What a relief! She didn't know his real name. The light from the campfire could not match the light of his smile.

Unlike his mother, he wasn't what anyone would mistake as a traditional redhead. His hair was a dark auburn with red undertones, or so his head sheet stated. His voluminous and lustrous hair was so integral to his look, the modeling agency even insisted he use a certain shampoo to accentuate those highlights. It could have been the angle of the firelight hitting the undertones, or perhaps it was his face, red with embarrassment. Whatever the reason, he could now forget about all his other names. Red Rover was perfect and using it would make the rest of the hike much easier.

Besides, as his uncle liked to say, everything was about context. Who would expect a famous tech billionaire to be hiking the Appalachian Trail solo?

Will reached the three-sided shelter of the Shady Pines campsite right on schedule. An Adirondack-type porch swing commanded a splendid view and dominated the spacious wooden deck that rested on a stack stone wall.

Since he had to be up at first light, and there didn't appear to be anyone around, it was tempting to keep things simple and bunk in the shelter. A closer look changed his mind. A small plastic bag and an opened bottle of soda on the sleeping platform gave the impression another hiker already claimed a spot.

Though it was first-come, first-served in the shelters, people couldn't reserve the whole space for themselves. In theory, the sleeping platforms were large enough to host three or four adults on sleeping bags, though during serious rains and other bad weather, more might try to cram in, depending on their comfort with the intimacy.

Will figured whoever owned the stuff probably wouldn't be spending the night since he saw no other camping equipment. And while he couldn't be sure, one thing was clear: Will would not share the space. The instructions strictly prohibited socializing after receiving an alert, and he'd already pushed his luck with a few pleasantries. Instead, he would sleep in his tent, cook up the last of his food, and hit the sack. The campsite was silent, except for the lone hoot of an owl, which reminded him how much he would miss the trail.

"Hey, Red Rover." The voice from the bottom of the steps startled him, but this time he recognized Streaming, a hiker he'd run into a few times in recent days. "You bunking here tonight? I thought you were going straight on through to Harpers Ferry."

"Yeah, a slight change of plans," Will explained. He remembered suggesting they hang out when they both got to the town. Streaming intended to turn around in Georgia and hike all the way back to Maine, called a "yo-yo" in trail parlance, and they both joked how non-hikers would consider it lunacy to take on the two-thousand-mile trek again. Oddly, Will felt envious.

He thought of how life-changing his adventure had been so far. The easiest hurdle was the physical one. A marathon like that required stamina, and he trained for it. But there were greater challenges, as he found early on. For the ten hours Will hiked every day, his brain had to go without emails, texts, reports, breaking news, and all the rest of the stuff that normally streamed through, so he didn't need training; he needed extensive behavior modification. It meant going cold turkey from the reliable euphoria a steady bombardment of data to scoring his sensory fix from actual sights and sounds and colors found in nature, not from pixels. It was a transition from a day planner that accounted for every fifteen minutes of his time, to a day planned around two events - sunrise and sunset.

Except for the occasional newspaper he picked up while shopping for provisions, the only communication with the outside world came through conversations with other hikers, and that's how he wanted it. He even designed his powerful watch without an email client or messaging capability and no way to browse the Internet. His ambition was to immerse himself in the Zen of Hiking, and features like those would have been irresistible not to use, making his goal unachievable.

It was far from the high-tech life that had brought him there, which started with a college applied science class where the assignment was to create an app. The professor stipulated that it couldn't be another game, and it had to be useful. He was thrilled with the assignment. His family had been preparing him for this his whole life. Will always gave credit for his brain being wired for innovation to his paternal grandfather who was an inventor. As a boy, he enjoyed many weekends building crazy inventions together in his workshop. Then, the summer before he started college, a last-minute slot became available at a science camp in Montreux, Switzerland, run by some colleagues of his uncle. The six-week "Nerd Camp," as Will referred to it, immersed him and eight other boys into the rarified world of advanced coding.

The idea for his project came to him at two in the morning when his roommate called Will for the third night in a row to let him in their dorm because he'd locked himself out. Will's invention was a gadget you attached to something you misplaced often, like a dorm keycard. Then with one click, his mobile app would locate the lost item on a map. He called it "The Doodad," and the first one off the production line went to his roommate. Soon everyone wanted one (or two) and before the end of the semester, he was selling hundreds online. The small company he had to form to handle production became a case study for another class he took on writing business plans.

The following summer he and his uncle, Alain, had a flash of genius to weave Will's technology into fabric, an idea that would change their lives forever. With seed money from his uncle, fabric became labels that could be sewn into clothing, and their vision was no longer limited to the misplaced car keys of forgetful teenagers. His small startup had made a big pivot, the ubiquitous industry buzzword referring to an important change in direction, and often a big change in revenue. They called their company GeoFibre, and through another of his uncle's connections they won a huge contract with the United States Department of Defense. Soon they stitched GeoFibre labels into every uniform throughout all branches of service, enabling the Pentagon to locate any service member anywhere on the globe virtually. From there, it was an easy lateral move into the burgeoning logistics industry, and soon both he and his uncle became billionaires.

When he studied pivoting in one of his college classes, he couldn't have known that his own experience would end up in Professor O'Shay's curriculum or that a building housing Entrepreneurial Studies would bear the de la Pomme name.

His mind wandered back to the talk show host and how he wished he'd never consented to do the interview.

"I wonder if people know you were born with a silver spoon in your mouth?" the talk show host continued. "An American actress for a mother, a European banker father and a life of privilege on both sides of the Atlantic. Glamorous boarding schools in Switzerland, a fancy college, all that."

"I'm guessing you didn't go to boarding school in Switzerland, did you, Gwen? If you had, I very much doubt you'd portray those years as glamorous." His loving parents raised him to be appreciative and never to act or even appear elitist. He insisted they led private lives.

"I guess what you call 'living a private life' is all relative." She winked to the studio audience again, and instantly the large backdrop screen and studio monitors filled with full-page ads and spreads showing Will as the face of one of the top luxury brands in the world.

He laughed. "Oh, come on. It was fun. I was just a teenager."

"Yes, but the ads ran for years," said Gwen, before returning to the question of how a rich person would celebrate becoming even richer.

"There's something I've wanted to do for a long time. Something money can't buy."

When she got the studio audience to beg for a little clue, he had some fun of his own.

Putting on a mysterious voice, he arched his brows. "Let's just say it will be very...low tech." He snickered when he recalled how she complimented him on his acting ability. "Thanks for noticing. Don't forget, it runs in the family," he laughed.

But now, alone on a mountain top in one of the most beautiful stretches of magnificence in the world, he had to put that low-tech adventure he promised himself on hold.

At least until he learned why his life was in such peril.

Chapter 4

Alain knew the custom ringtone on Suzen Movora's phone would be enough to ensure she picked up right away. It was ten o'clock in the evening for her, and since he lived in Geneva, which was six hours ahead, the four a.m. call would appear even more urgent. Suzen and Will had been working side by side for eight years, first as his longtime assistant and then as the President of GeoFibre Foundation. While he understood the affection and trust they had for each other, he could not say the same about his own relationship with Suzen. While they were always cordial, and she always showed him the utmost respect, she didn't know the slightest thing about him.

What she did know was that he owned a major interest in GeoFibre with Will and was one of two people whose calls she was required to take. Beyond that, Alain made sure that what he did outside GeoFibre was vague. Most GeoFibre employees assumed he worked as some sort of advertising or public relations consultant, and they all knew he was prone to disappearing for long, unexplained stretches. He liked Suzen, but he was comfortable with the emotional distance between them and chalked it up to another of the challenges of coming from different cultures and living in different hemispheres.

When she answered his call, he acknowledged it was probably a bad time and promised not to keep her long. She brushed off any worry about disturbing her and automatically gave him a thumbnail of her trip. He stopped her mid-sentence. There was no time for small talk. The reason for the call was urgent.

"Listen. I initiated Plan B."

Plan B was the contingency system put in place to rescue Will and different from the SOS system built in his watch that he could activate at any time. Prior to leaving, all three of them established rules for Plan B's implementation. Only Suzen and Alain were authorized to launch it, but extraordinary and grave circumstances needed to exist for either to trigger it on their own.

"What on earth happened?"

"I'll explain in a minute," he said. "In the meantime, I need to get Will to safety."

"Safety? Good lord, well of course!" She paused. "At least locating him will be easy. We always know exactly where he is."

Alain cleared his throat. "I'm afraid that's the problem. We don't."

"What? Why not?"

"While you were traveling, for some reason those alerts that only you and I receive stopped being sent. With everything on your plate, I didn't expect you to notice."

A long silence followed as she scrolled frantically through her email, searching for the ones that gave her Will's daily location. "What? Wait, here it is. You're right, the last one I have is dated the day before I left the country."

"Exactly. Mine, too."

Suzen tried to reassure him that Dillon, the office manager, had committed to keep an eye on Will while she was away and suggested missing emails was probably not serious. She promised to call Dillon first thing in the morning.

"I'm afraid it can't wait until tomorrow," said Alain. "I called the office several times that day, and no one ever answered. Worse yet, nobody returned my call, so I knew something was wrong."

To prepare for Will's hike, the guys in the lab sewed GeoFibre labels in his clothing and gear, so his New York office could track their valuable boss. From the start of his hike, Will's exact location bounced off satellites from the labels twenty-four seven. Moment by moment, his elevation, speed, and rest times synthesized with other data and streamed to a huge digital 3D map of the trail that occupied one long wall. They selected the conference room between Suzen and Will's offices as the map room for its privacy, as the constantly updating arrays and overlays of flashing lights and numbers were intended to dazzle only a few privileged pairs of eyes. Will was fanatical about keeping his whereabouts under wraps so he could experience the adventure as a private citizen. He couldn't have predicted the anonymity would protect him from someone trying to find and kill him.

While the location and weather data would come in handy later for the memoir Will planned to pen, a significant aspect of the low-tech adventure was keeping a diary. Every night before going to sleep, without fail, he made an entry. Though he complained about how challenging it would be, he had the discipline. Part of the rigor of his boarding school experience included keeping a journal, and while he never dropped the routine, the mechanics changed on the trail. Prior to the hike, an app converted his voice to text, then date-stamped and stored his thoughts in the Cloud. What he faced on the trail was reverting to the original method — writing in a real notebook with an actual pen.

It wasn't the only manual daily record being kept. Alain

insisted on a human interface as an extra safeguard to the data-driven procedure. Each day at the same time, Dillon was to enter Will's coordinates in a physical notebook and then manually send an encrypted email alert to Alain and Suzen, pinpointing Will's exact location.

Alain knew the conversation with Suzen would be horribly upsetting, and he considered giving her the elevator speech, so he could keep it short and a little vague. He contemplated throwing in a few alternative facts for good measure, since he wasn't at liberty to share many real ones.

"I don't understand. What's happened?" she asked.

"A combination of things." He reconsidered his original intentions and confessed to being brought in to consult on a situation developing in New York. Something about an unsavory character, maybe an assassin, running around causing a little mischief, and how Alain stumbled across bits and pieces of information that led to a few suspicions and theories.

Before he got further, she interrupted him. "What are you talking about? Bits and pieces? I stopped listening after 'assassin.' You are making me very nervous. Why are you telling me about him?"

"See, the authorities don't know exactly who he or she is, but his *modus operandi* reminds them of another high-profile guy people used to call Le Mauvais." Then he asked offhandedly, "Maybe you've heard of him?"

"What? You're talking about that monster who went around breaking people's necks? Of course, I've heard of him. He was in the news all the time. This is the character you're referring to as unsavory? I thought he was dead."

"No, no. Sorry, I didn't mean to mislead you. This is someone new, a sort of copycat killer." He tried to avoid going into any more detail by suggesting it was a long, complicated and probably boring story.

"There is nothing remotely boring about a maniac hitman

running around the city." She sat down. "Okay. I'm going to ask again. What does he have to do with Will and Plan B?"

He paused. "Apparently, this assassin has finished his work in New York. They believe he's headed for the Appalachian Trail."

"What? We can't have Will out there with some killer on the loose. Now I'm glad you didn't listen when I complained that all those precautions of yours were overkill. Thanks to those contingency plans, we'll have him out in no time. What a relief!" She paused. "Wait a minute. A moment ago, you said 'you' needed to get him to safety. What's that supposed to mean? Don't we have real professionals standing by?"

"I was serious. But I don't blame you for asking," he replied. "I probably forgot to tell you that this type of thing is part of my skill set."

"I'm sorry. Your skill set? Look, Alain. I know you are my boss, and I might be crossing a line here, but I don't care. Do you have any idea how nerve-wracking this conversation is? I need you to explain everything right now in simple English. No more baloney."

"Okay, Suzen. I'll give it to you straight. It's not just that there's a killer. It's conceivable that he or she is after Will. It's also possible someone in the office didn't want us to know where Will is so they could locate him first."

"I feel like all this is my fault." She jumped to her feet. "I'm on my way to the office!" She snapped off the lights, grabbed her purse, and bolted out of her apartment.

Chapter 5

"Want help with yer tent?"

It was the same voice that startled Will an hour earlier, and for the second time it came from behind. Will jumped, embarrassed for being so easily unnerved and skittish from the alert and its inferred danger. But the guy seemed to sneak up on him deliberately. Either way, Will wanted to keep his cool.

"Thanks, but nah. I've got one of these crazy simple tents. They practically set up themselves."

"Sweet. Can I see?"

"Okay, I guess."

Pitching the tent was one of Will's favorite parts of setting up camp because it was so insanely fast. All wrapped up, his tent measured only a meter long and a few centimeters around. Frustrated at fitting everything back in the matching bag every morning, he ditched it long ago. Another hiker he met along the way said the bag would be perfect for something she needed, so he gave it to her. That was how recycling worked among hikers. Now, he only needed one bungee cord to hold everything together.

According to the code his uncle sent to his watch, whatever

he had to worry about was still ten hours away, so the hiker standing so close to him didn't fit as part of the problem. But, as soon as he finished his demonstration, he would establish boundaries. That part of the protocol was clear: *After receiving an alert, don't engage with anyone.*

"Like I said, there's really nothing to it." Will took three steps to one side to create space between them. "Watch this." He pulled up on a cord and the bundle unpacked itself and became a tent. The whole process took seconds.

The hiker stepped back into Will's space. "How does it go back down?"

Will continued the dance and retreated a few paces. "Easy and almost as fast. You just pull off these top hubs and straighten out the legs." He regretted letting the guy draw him into conversation.

"Sweet!" The hiker paused. "Show me."

"Well, I'm obviously not going to show you now, but if you're up early enough, you can watch me take it down tomorrow morning."

"I'm gerna get me one of them."

"They're pretty cheap." Will was grateful that his mother made him spend so many summers in the states. Like his uncle, he'd developed a flawless New England accent at a young age, and he marveled how he and this native-born American might as well have been speaking different languages. "You can get them online," he mumbled, avoiding eye contact.

The hiker's expression was blank. "Online?"

Will considered the unlikelihood of a so-called tech superstar running into one of the thirteen percent of adults who still didn't use the Internet. But he had a lot on his mind, and what he needed was to eat something and squeeze in as much sleep as he could within the short time left. He deliberately turned his back to the hiker and started to gather firewood.

The strategy was successful. Without another word, the

hiker crossed the clearing and climbed the steps to the sleeping platform where he fished around in the little daypack and produced a candy bar. Then he plopped down on the wooden porch swing. It gave a loud creak in resistance and cried out louder when he leaned back. Will watched him grab the chains and swing like a child, with both legs in the air. The links ground and squeaked with each pass. Back and forth. Steady rhythm. *Squeak, squeak.* As he swung, his eyes never stopped watching Will work.

"They say you're Red Rover." The guy's delivery was flat and without affect. But as weird as his brush was with the creep, Will thought the encounter would make a scary chapter in his book. In the meantime, he ignored him. Fortunately, he didn't have to look up to know he was still swinging. The creaking noise kept him informed. The guy was probably still staring, too, but Will was grateful that at least he wasn't lurking over his shoulder.

Will's last supper would be larger than normal because he had shopped recently, and he didn't want to waste anything. Besides, he could easily restock his provisions in Harpers Ferry after he resolved whatever was so serious that they made him take a break from his hike.

In the meantime, he was comfortable on the log facing the fire quietly stirring garlic and onions as his pasta water came to a boil. The sizzle and aroma never failed to elevate his mood, and he smiled as it reminded him of something the family cook used to say when he was a young boy hanging around in the kitchen. "It doesn't matter what you're going to cook, François, always start by sautéing some onions."

His mind wandered back to what could be serious enough to trigger Plan B. His uncle had the authority to act on Will's behalf, so it likely wasn't a business issue. Alain had been supportive of Will's adventure and would never interrupt it frivolously.

The onions were ready, and while he waited for the noodles to cook, he decided to write the day's first entry in his journal. He knew there wouldn't be enough time to express his thoughts on everything that had occurred, so he began with something fun. He wrote about his kooky encounter with the strange hiker.

But writing didn't come easy. For two-and-a-half months he'd practiced focusing on the moment and developing a peaceful mind, so when the time came to write about his feelings and impressions, the ink had always flowed. Suddenly now, his mind was anything but peaceful. Random chatter filled his head and clamored for his brain's attention, blocking his thoughts. Some yogic breathing exercises helped but only temporarily.

He put his pen down. Something wasn't right. He looked around and didn't see anything out of the ordinary. It wasn't a noise that interrupted his train of thought because there was none - and that was the problem. There was no squeaking. The swing hung empty and motionless, and he wondered how long ago it stopped. He saw no sign of the guy, either, and he hoped he'd finally taken the hint and left. All the same, not knowing gave him an uncomfortable chill.

"Boo," laughed the hiker, startling Will from behind.

No question the guy intentionally snuck up on him.

"I passed you on the trail," the guy said again, as though it was the first time.

Will continued to stare into the fire, pretending not to make the connection or care. "Oh, was that you?"

"Maybe," teased the hiker.

The way the guy repeated things made Will believe he was dealing with someone who wasn't all there, and it was unnerving. He was unprepared with strategies to transact socially with a person like that, and he worried he would say or do the wrong thing. Hissing from the pot where the noodles were burning interrupted their conversation, and he instinctively yanked the pot off the fire and dumped water into it from his canteen.

"I guess dinner's ready," Will grumbled, somewhat glad for the distraction.

"Can I have some?"

As he strained the noodles with his fork and mixed in the vegetables, Will decided it was best to ignore him. The hiker moved closer. He pointed at the food and asked him again, this time louder. When he ignored the guy before, it only provoked him, so he tried another tactic.

"Um, sure, I guess. I cooked way too much, anyway. It's a little burned, though. Got a bowl?"

"No."

"Well, okay. Here, you can use mine." Will would eat directly out of the pot.

"You got sumthin' to eat this with?"

Reluctantly, Will handed over his only fork.

It was clear to Will that he was not a hiker. The guy was unequipped with the basics, and now, besides being annoyed, Will was alarmed. He found it difficult to eat with the mindfulness he'd developed over the past months, and instead he wolfed down his food as he considered his next move.

"Say, friend," Will started, "if we are going to share this campsite, we should at least know each other's name. For some reason you know mine, ha ha, but I don't know yours."

The guy grinned. "Yeah, you're Red Rover." He inched closer.

It was more than an invasion of his personal space and the crazy repetition again. Will could hear his own heart beating. It was time to put an end to the drama, and he decided to change the scene. He stood abruptly and announced that he was off to refill his canteen from the water pump behind the shelter. Then he would wash everything and turn in. Since the guy had already gotten a free meal, Will thought perhaps he'd lose interest and leave if Will stayed out of sight long enough.

Staring at his watch to kill time was more challenging than he'd expected, especially since the only other thing to look at was the pump, but it gave him another idea. After ten minutes, he shuddered when he saw what was waiting. Not only was the guy still sitting at the fire, he was wearing Will's coat.

"Cold," the hiker said with a big smile, as though that one word would explain everything.

"Sorry. I'm afraid you can't have that." Will put on a guy-to-guy voice that would sound firm, without being threatening. "It's the only one I've got, and I need it myself tonight."

"Cold," the hiker repeated. This time he locked his arms across his chest, daring Will to take it.

"Yeah, I'm cold, too. So, please hand it over now, will you?"

Will's demand met with silence, the sound of a standoff. "I've something else to keep you warm," he said as he produced a tiny plastic pouch from an outer pocket of his backpack. "Yeah, you will love this."

The guy's eyes lit up when Will removed the shiny metallic space blanket, and his thick fingers tore it from Will's hand. He seemed fascinated and for the next few minutes he struggled to unfold it. He held it up, not seeming to know what to do.

"It's a blanket," Will said. "You can wrap it around you."

The hiker gurgled a sound Will interpreted as satisfaction. "Good. Glad you like it. I'll trade it with you for my coat."

Defiantly, the hiker draped the thin blanket over his shoulders directly on top of Will's jacket and frowned back at Will. His gurgle turned to a growl.

Will stared in disbelief. "You know, go ahead. Keep them both. No need to give it back. Okay?"

The guy pointed to Will's backpack. "Gimme that, too."

"Hey, friend, look. I'm not sure how far you want to take this, but I think it's time you went back to your spot over there." He stood and gestured toward the shelter.

"No," came the calm response. Then he shouted. "Sit back down!"

The force of his command was startling, and Will immediately obeyed. Did his uncle know about this guy running around loose? Could he be the reason they were calling him off the trail? He reminded himself the timing of the guy's appearance was wrong. Will had twelve more hours left. Still, the threat he posed was happening right now in real time, and he had read enough horror books to know that unstable and unpredictable crazy persons were about the scariest thing in the world.

Suddenly, a sharp beam of light temporarily blinded him. It had passed across his face and landed directly in his eyes. Will blocked the annoyance with his hand and traced its source to light from the campfire reflecting on the long shiny blade of Will's hunting knife, which was now in the hiker's possession. The guy held it in his lap and was tilting it so the beam crossed back and forth between Will's eyes.

Will thought his knife looked more menacing in the other guy's hands because the creep looked like someone who knew how to use it, and Will hoped robbery was all he had in mind. He was not eager for a fight, but if it came down to a scuffle, at least they were about the same size, and more or less evenly matched.

But Will wasn't a fighter, and he backed down. "Look, buddy. There's no need to get rough. You want my backpack? Take it. It's yours."

The guy reached over and yanked it by the straps. Once in his hands, he hugged it like a child with a toy he didn't want to share.

"Okay, then. Well, that's settled." Will faked a yawn. "Man, I'm tired. Why don't we both just turn in now?"

The hiker wasn't finished. He waved the knife and demanded Will's tent and the rest of his gear. He even wanted his sweater. Pulling it off exposed his watch, which caught the guy's attention, and Will had to turn that over, too. Will's heart was thumping, as he realized he'd have to relinquish everything to get out alive.

"I hope you'll at least let me keep my pants on," he stammered.

"Yeah."

The guy patted him down, and Will was glad he kept his cash zipped up in one of the secret cargo pockets. Holding the knife in his teeth, the hiker bound Will's hands using one of Will's bungee cords, and, convinced he'd rendered him helpless; the guy focused his attention on his new toy, Will's Epix. Just by grazing the screen with a fat finger, dials and buttons appeared out of nowhere. He'd never seen a watch like this before, and he was intrigued. He poked at random icons not knowing the use, complexity, or the power of their functions.

As they sat together facing the fire, Will's back was getting cold since the hiker had confiscated his t-shirt, as well. Now all he could think of was how he would escape from this madman. He faked a smile as he pretended to cooperate, but soon the smile turned authentic, when he realized he had a plan. "Want me to show you how to use it? It can do some neat tricks."

"Okay, but don't try nothing." He reminded Will who was in charge when he pointed to the knife, which now was on the ground at his side.

"Don't worry. There's not much I can do with my hands tied together like this."

The hiker passed the watch back. Navigating was awkward, but he demonstrated its features well enough using only his thumbs, pushing buttons and activating counters and sweep hands. One icon brought up a map.

"See where this green dot is blinking?" he said, tilting the watch face in the guy's direction. "It's where we are right now." The map didn't seem to interest him. In fact, none of the functions seemed to keep his attention, and Will was afraid of losing him. He tried another tactic.

A few finger swipes brought up a colorful layout of a farm on the watch's face. He started a new game and soon pumpkins with giant chomping teeth chased a farmer around his property. Will explained that you were supposed to keep the farmer away from them, and the longer you kept him from being bitten, the more pumpkins appeared out of nowhere and added to the chase. The guy laughed, as fascinated by Will's thumbs dancing on the screen as by the pumpkins that snapped at the farmer in the game. He leaned in.

With his captor completely intrigued, Will asked if he'd like to take a crack at playing the game himself. The hiker nodded. Will stopped playing and pushed another button. "Here, let me show you how."

Slowly he held the watch by the dial and prepared to hand it over. But the guy didn't wait, and he grabbed it. The moment it left Will's hands, the custom Epix let out a high-pitched and piercing *screech*, startling them both. The noise grew louder, and the guy shook his head and covered his ears, more frightened than confused. When suddenly a dizzying strobe light shot out of the dial and created more confusion and panic, he squeezed his eyes shut. He was unprepared for the uppercut Will delivered to his chin with his wrists. Bound together they made a powerful weapon, and he followed the first jab by plowing them into the guy's nose. After several more blows to the back of his head, the guy finally keeled over. When the watch dropped out of his thick fingers and landed on the ground, it fell silent.

Will groped in the dark for his knife and cut his hands free. It would be difficult to find his way through the forest, but he didn't care. The guy looked unconscious and Will finally had the advantage. While the guy was out, Will could make his escape. It was now or never.

Too late. The man was slapping his head. When he went

down, his head landed near the fire, and the sparks singed his scalp. A few more slaps to his burning hair revived him enough to see Will's back as he was preparing to leave. When he stuck out a leg and tripped Will, the tables turned.

Scrambling to his feet, Will grabbed the only weapon he could see. Gripping his fork, he gulped as he faced his opponent who held a log like a club in one hand and Will's knife in the other.

Chapter 6

LATER

The approach was skillful. Slow and steady. Each foot placed expertly on the forest floor as precisely as the one before. They didn't make a sound. Not one snap of a twig or crackle of a leaf.

Like a Geiger counter sensing ionizing radiation, the small handheld gadget that zeroed in on its prey resembled an older iPod, but this device wasn't playing music. The beeping sounds sent through the earbuds told the user the victim was dead ahead. Even with the fancy gadget, having someone on the inside eager to help was invaluable to get them to the general location. All that remained was to fine-tune the search with the scanner. After pinpointing the target, the rest would be over in minutes.

And there he sat, alone on a log facing the other way, silhouetted by the campfire. What a dope! The tech big shot would never see it coming.

The rapid-fire beeps marked that it was time for visual corroboration. The light from the fire made him a cinch to verify, even from behind. Tall, check. Black jacket, check. According to the insider, his backpack would be absinthe green. *What the hell kind of green is that?* Anyway, the pack was definitely some kind of green, so yeah, check. Both were supposed to be expensive, too. They probably were, but how could you tell? Not that it mattered anyway. The device was failsafe, designed uniquely to identify this man. Paired with the daily log of his location, it ensured there would be no mistake, and after all, the assassin didn't want to waste their talents on someone who didn't deserve it.

Time to put on the gloves. This part of the job would be a snap. Literally. Only a few more silent steps remained before the guy would be close enough to touch. The assassin positioned practiced hands strategically on either side of the unsuspecting victim's head. In one split second, they clamped down. *Crack!* The head flopped down, and the now dead man's chin struck his chest. *Nothing to it.*

In the firelight, a few of the victim's belongings caught the assassin's eye. The watch was easily pried from the dead man's wrist, and the corpse forfeited the sweater it would no longer need. On the way out, the assassin threw the gloves in the fire and as an afterthought, tossed the device at the fire, too. *Wouldn't want to get caught with that!*

The killer took off up the path at a healthy jogging pace, which quickly became a run. The departure, while not as stealthy as the arrival, didn't need to be. Phase One complete.

Chapter 7

"Glad I caught you before you left. Is this a good time?"

Alain recognized Major M's serious business voice and was glad to be nursing a glass of Bordeaux. "Yes, but I did leave already. I'm on the GeoFibre plane headed for New York, so I have plenty of time to talk."

"Not a moment too soon. I've got a troubling new development, and it concerns you."

"How bad could it be? Lay it on me."

Without missing a beat, Major M dropped the bomb. "You're the target, Alain. We just heard from one of our plants who hide out in those dark places we monitor. He's been following conversations between two individuals who we presume are Le Mauvais and his surrogate."

"Look, there are plenty of characters who would like to see both of us pay for bringing them in. I've had to look over my shoulder all my life. But what makes you think it's me?"

"Lots of reasons. We're also seeing the word 'revenge.' I'm afraid it's loud and clear. And damn if Le Mauvais isn't good at covering his cyber tracks. We still can't trace them, and it's what we do around here."

"Okay, I'll buy that you think he's after me, but none of the rest of this makes sense." Alain was relieved to hear that he was the target, and not his nephew, but it made the assassin's use of the trail confusing. "Why is this guy looking for me on the Appalachian Trail?"

"Good question. We're double checking the data because obviously, we got it wrong." He chuckled. "Unless you've suddenly taken up hiking."

Alain pressed a button on his armrest and the steward appeared. Alain pointed to his empty glass, and the young man returned with a wine bottle. "Now you've got me thinking Le Mauvais slipped through your fingers, and it's him after all."

"I wish I hadn't put that thought in your head. I told you, we have a tight lid on the place.

We don't doubt for a moment that he is calling the shots, but he's doing it from somewhere in Thailand. It's his accomplice who is after you."

"Do you have any idea if I know this guy? Somebody you and I met before?"

"First, you've got to stop referring to the accomplice as a he. At this stage, we can't assume anything."

Alain took another sip. "Revenge is a pretty popular pastime. I'd like to believe you, but it seems to me, if you're wrong about the Appalachian Trail, you could be wrong about me being the one they're after."

"We're not. I was hoping I wouldn't have to argue the point, so let me lay it all out for you. The encryptions from both sides contain the letters DLP. And if that's not enough to convince you, we also found mentions of GeoFibre."

Alain stopped sipping and took a long gulp. "Is it possible you all misinterpreted the intel, and it's my nephew they're after? He's a de la Pomme, too."

Major M long ago decided not to call Alain's nephew

William or François and settled on using both names together. "William François? Why him? You'd be the one to avenge. Anyway, I doubt Will's any closer to the Appalachian Trail than you are."

"But that's where you're wrong. He's hiking the trail at this very moment."

There was a pause at the other end of the line. "Good God, Alain! Why didn't you tell me? Forget the assassin for now. We've got to get William François off that trail pronto."

"It's why I left early."

"Well, I guess we can assume he's wearing those magic labels of yours, so he'll be easy to find."

Alain declined the offer of a refill. It was an extraordinary Bordeaux, but he'd need to be sharp for what was coming. "Yes, certainly. But I have to confess that something's recently gone haywire with his tracking system. I hoped it was only a glitch, but I'm afraid it's far worse."

"Doesn't sound like a coincidence to me. William François is the closest thing I have to a nephew. We don't have a moment to lose. Any idea where he is?"

Until a week ago, they knew his exact location, and since Will had been more or less sticking to his itinerary, they only needed to concern themselves with a hundred-mile stretch.

"Great, then under the circumstances do you think you could work up a few rescue scenarios? You were always better at planning than I was. Assume you'll have everything you need."

"We're way ahead of you. I'll send you the detailed plans we put together before he left. We have a Plan B, too, which may give us an advantage. It should even impress you."

The moment he received the Plan B alert, Will was to swallow two capsules. The first contained an experimental nano-transmitter designed to signal his rescue team. Since the device would end up in his stomach, it needed to be self-powered, so a second capsule contained a nanogenerator, which was not experimental. In both tests and in practice, vibration-driven nanogenerators could scavenge mechanical vibrations from all over the human body and turn them into electricity, and they didn't require much. Scientists had built them to be self-powered from something as subtle as the vibrations of a person's own blood flow, which was how it would operate in Will's body.

What was new in Plan B was a larger capacitor, one that would store enough energy to transmit its signals farther than previous models. In actual experiments, the maximum distance other scientists had transmitted a signal using a similar device was thirty feet. The GeoFibre lab had successfully tripled the distance, and with the improvements in Plan B, they hoped to reach over a hundred yards, which would add a significant advantage for search and rescue through a dense forest on a steep mountain trail in the dark.

Will was so fascinated by the implications of this technology in surveillance and medicine, he became a major investor in the leading company in the field. His hike created a real-time opportunity to test their advanced nanotechnology and a perfect excuse to be a test subject.

"You're right. I am impressed," Major M said. "I've been following advancements in that type of nanotech since the beginning and had no idea you were so far ahead of everyone else."

"Well, this is where things fall apart. For Plan B to work, we need to be within less than a mile of his location. We sent Will's watch the signal to abort his hike, and his return confirmation would have given us his exact coordinates. Since we didn't get it, we can't be sure he even received the alert."

"You mean Will might not be aware he's in trouble."

"That's right. My imagination has been running wild, and

I'm worried something horrible may have happened to him. I was on my way to rescue him myself when you called just now."

"Then I'm glad I did. Look, old friend. I'm not letting you go at this yourself. William François is an important figure to the business world, and it will be easy to justify, if I have to. Like I said, I'll provide all the resources you'd need, and we'll even do the heavy lifting. We've got this, Alain."

Each of his contingency plans required additional personnel and assets, and now with the manpower and the agency's equipment at his disposal, implementing any of them would be easier. He was glad Major M offered them before Alain had to ask.

But Major M had another shoe to drop. They would still need to bring in the hitman. "Given that Will is now part of the equation, are you still interested?"

His question was not unexpected.

"We both know the next obligatory conversation. Yes, François is the most important person in my life. I always said that when my brother died, he left me Will as his parting gift. So, no, I can't imagine anything more personal."

"I know, but--"

"You want my assurance it won't cloud my thinking. It won't. I believe I've demonstrated many times I can compartmentalize. Now can we get on with it?"

Finding someone who wouldn't want to be found in the middle of the vast Appalachian Trail added significantly to the difficulty and the risk, but he and Major M had a lifetime of covert rescue operation experience in areas that were equally remote. In those cases, though, they at least had descriptions of the people they were searching for. To date, Major M could not provide Alain with anything helpful.

In spite of being away from the agency for nearly two years, Alain kept a bag packed and ready out of habit. He preferred to travel light, and his custom was to pick up whatever else he needed wherever they sent him.

Like the many scenarios he put together before, this one would reliably be in a state of flux. Extracting someone from the wilderness was tricky enough. Here, the target would be moving. *Targets*, technically. His nephew was the easy one. Everyone would have his description, and he'd be expecting rescuers looking for him. All they had on the assassin was that William François was the target.

Major M added one more wrinkle. It was crucial to keep the entire mission a secret, so Alain would have to accomplish both aims without attracting attention. Closing the trail wasn't an option; it would have the opposite effect because it would inevitably raise questions and generate rumors, which hikers would find irresistible to spread. Not only would that jeopardize the mission, it would be a public relations nightmare for the National Park Service.

"Any idea how Le Mauvais would know that William François was hiking the trail?" Major M asked. "He isn't the type to publicize his vacation."

"That is the question I've been wracking my brain to figure out."

"I guess you must reconcile to the possibility of a security breach at GeoFibre, won't you?"

"Yes, and it breaks my heart to think of it." He hung up the phone.

Alain had been staring at the ocean for about an hour, running through every possible iteration of his plan, when something suddenly came to him. He tapped out a directive to the pilot. In seconds, he felt the plane bank in response to the new flight plan.

When the jet's descent awakened Alain later, he gazed out at the sprawling Suvarnabhumi airport below and smiled. He loved the city from his first visit and never tired of walking its mysterious streets. This time he was staying only long enough to meet with one person, and how much time he needed depended on traffic. Bangkok was notorious for its gridlock.

Fortunately, Alain's regular driver would be waiting. He really knew his way around the city and where to find the best noodles. Alain counted on him knowing how to get his hands on some other information, too.

Chapter 8

The luxurious furnishings of the GeoFibre jet maximized the comfort for every trip, but flights between Asia and New York always left Suzen exhausted and simultaneously wide awake. After a week of intense negotiations and back-to-back conferences, she had looked forward to spending the night in her own bed. It was just after eleven in the evening when she entered her office at the GeoFibre Foundation on Eighth Avenue in Times Square.

Though she and Will had loved the fast-paced environment at GeoFibre, she always thought spinning off the Foundation was one of the best decisions they made. Doing good work around the world gave them both an added sense of purpose, and the publicity for GeoFibre was a nice bonus. With Will off on his adventure, it left Suzen to manage things on her own, and she was alarmed at the idea that something had gone wrong under her watch.

One quick look around put her mind at ease. Based on Alain's dire revelations, she didn't anticipate finding the office in pristine condition. Other than two stacks of unopened mail and a few packages piled on the floor in the reception area, it looked as though Dillon had been following procedures. The office reflected Will's love of order at every turn. *A place for everything, and everything in its place* was not only an axiom his maternal grandfather drilled into him at a young age, it was engraved on a plaque. The special keepsake now hung above the sink in the staff kitchen daring any employee to leave a mess. An opened box of chocolates on the counter caught her eye. Everyone in the office knew of Dillon's fondness for them, and she made a mental note of the company's name and its foreign address so she would know what to buy him for his birthday.

It was dark and quiet except for the gentle whirring of some electronic thingamajig or another cycling on and off. The sounds apparently made some of her staff uncomfortable on those occasions when they worked alone at night, but they never bothered her. During those frantic early startup days, she and Will spent so many crazy late nights there, it always felt like a second home, and when they spun off from the rest of the company, she was adamant about keeping the GeoFibre Foundation in the original space.

She liked the way Will referred to her as his "right-hand arm," an expression the press loved to repeat. She was smart, a quick study, and she'd been with him from the start. As GeoFibre grew, she'd grown with it. Now, after ten years together, he trusted her with everything. She even learned to speak decent French.

She heard a beep that signaled her coffee was ready, and she carried it into her suite. The Foundation operated with a relatively small staff, and she and Will were the only ones to have large private offices. There were a few dedicated workspaces, but they shared administrative support with the main company on the floor below. Everyone else, though, either worked from home, on the road, or shared the few workspace "hotels" scattered throughout the suite. Such was the current trend in office design. A large conference room occupied the space between her suite and Will's, accessible from each of their offices. For the duration of Will's hike, that space served as the map room.

She didn't bother turning on her lights. Instead, she headed directly for her sofa. She'd delve into the alert issue in a minute. In the meantime, the cool leather felt soothing on the back of her neck. Sinking in deeper, she felt herself beginning to relax. She was sleepier now than an hour ago when she told Alain she was on her way. Her mind wandered, and soon her eyelids drooped. If she wasn't careful, she knew she might nod off, and to prevent that adjusted her body and sat up straight. Still, the soft leather and the quiet darkness felt overpowering, and her body sagged with fatigue. In a moment, she was out.

Her chin struck her chest, and she jerked upright. Terrified of the close call, she groped in the dark on the side sofa table for her coffee mug. She took a long slug. Caffeine reliably kept her awake, and she knew it was safe to lean back again while it kicked in. When she was more alert, she would examine the log for the lapse in protocol. She hoped Will's uncle Alain was being overly dramatic and unnecessarily worried, and that she'd find a reasonable explanation.

It was soothing sitting in the darkness alone, and she closed her eyes again to focus on positive thoughts. Suddenly she sat up. Something was very wrong. A glance at the glass wall separating her office from the map room made her leap to her feet and spill her coffee. It was never totally dark in the map room. Where were the flashing lights and data scrawls? She dashed into the black conference room and, switching on the lights, darted straight for the leather-bound alert log. After flipping through two or three pages, she raced back to her desk, where she placed her first call to GeoFibre's Chief Technology Officer. When he and a few of his team arrived, she made the second call to Alain.

Suzen shared with him what the engineers discovered. Someone disabled the entire satellite system dedicated to tracking Will, which was why no feeds went out for several days.

"He told me it was definitely sabotaged, Alain. It's a real mess and will take them a while just to figure out what happened. Impossible to estimate how long to get it back up and running."

Trying to sound upbeat, she added, "Luckily, the damage seems to be confined here in the map room and affected none of our mainframes. Excuse me for a minute, please."

"That's a relief," said Alain.

In fifteen seconds, she was back, with a message from her team. "They said they can fix it. They don't know how long it will take, but they said there is no reason to worry."

"I wish I shared their optimism," he said. Then he dropped the bomb.

"Will is the assassin's target.

"Are you kidding? Why would someone want to hurt him?"

"I can't get into the details, but the motivation has more to do with me than with him."

"But we can still get him out, right? You said you initiated Plan B."

"I did. It's just that we never got a confirmation signal back from him, so things are more complicated than we expected. Oh, and there's something else. I wanted you to know that I'm here."

"So, are you meeting me here in the office?"

"No, I don't mean New York. I meant I'm here, in the field."

"In the field?" His ability to be vague no longer surprised her.

"Yes, Harpers Ferry, West Virginia."

Chapter 9

Alain hung up the phone, wishing he could have shared more with Suzen. Not being able to talk about his wild and exciting former day job with friends and loved ones was a tradeoff he'd lived with for decades and contributed to his chronic sense of detachment and loneliness.

Thanks to Major M, Alain was able to deploy dozens of drones to scour for humans on the trail. When they spotted one, they relayed the coordinates to agents on the ground who rounded them up, one by one. Fortunately for Alain, there were only a few, but unfortunately, Will was not among them. For the drone cameras to have missed him, Alain figured he must have stopped moving. He prayed the reason was because Will was sleeping under a tree and not the alternative, which was unthinkable. Finding his nephew called for more than technology. He'd need his wits.

According to the master itinerary, Will was to overnight at the Shady Pines campsite the day Alain sent the alert. Even when they were tracking him, they noticed he hadn't stuck precisely to his plan, but the campsite was a logical place to start for another reason. The Montreux lab finally received Will's Plan B confirmation signal, and though the technicians couldn't explain the reason for the considerable delay in ping, they determined the signal originated less than five miles away from the campsite.

Alain and a member of his team surveilled the area from the woods through night goggles. He wore his black tactical suit, which always reminded him of his childhood dream of growing up to be a Ninja. This night, he was neither as young nor as agile as the character of his imagination, yet the outfit always gave him extra confidence. Major M came through, and teams were already in place at the right locations. He had every conceivable tool at his disposal.

"I don't expect to find Will here, but I hope we can discover some clues," he said to Alvaro, his favorite colleague, and one who had accompanied him on missions many times before.

There had been no activity at the campground since he arrived, which he took as a sign that clearing the trail was working. He concocted a story about a large family of aggressive bears, and he deployed a batch of fake rangers for one hundred miles on either side of the campground to spread the story. The idea was to encourage hikers to exit the trail voluntarily at Harpers Ferry. To sweeten the pot, the rangers offered coupons for free accommodations. If they met with resistance, the fake rangers were to ratchet up the tale to scare them into compliance. If that still didn't work, they had instructions to use whatever means they needed to remove the hikers. Fortunately, it had not been necessary to implement those means.

They spread out combing the campsite using a double helix formation, from the outside in, ending at the campfire. Alain investigated the area around the campfire. Someone had organized a cooking pot and utensils in front of one of the log seats. He saw a pot tipped on its side and an unwashed bowl and spoon on the ground nearby. He sniffed at the burned remains of food in the pot.

"I was there when Will bought his cook set, and these pots

look like his. Ordinarily, I'd say that would be enough proof," he said to Alvaro, "but he would never have left dishes lying around, washed or unwashed, so they likely belong to someone else. I just can't be sure."

The Swiss would consider the mess litter and therefore appalling. The full canteen added another layer of mystery. There was more than enough water to extinguish the fire. He wanted to believe an irresponsible camper left the campsite in this disturbing condition, but the dirt surrounding the fire showed evidence of a major scuffle, and he couldn't deny a sinking feeling in his gut.

"Either this is someone else's setup, or Will's in trouble. He would never leave a fire burning without supervision."

When they first arrived, they noticed something emitting an amber light outside the main ring of ashes and assumed it was an outlier ember. Through the goggles, the color appeared different, and its light pulsed in a regular pattern. Alvaro went to inspect.

"Here's that thing we saw," Alvaro said, poking at the object with a long stick. "It's definitely something custom-made."

With its connected earbuds and a single button, the object on the ground resembled an early iPod. Heat from the fire melted the plastic earbud wires in places but had not charred the case. Alain had no idea if the gizmo was related to the assassin or simply the property of a random and forgetful hiker. Either way, he'd get it checked out right away at their lab. If the heat hadn't damaged the insides too badly, he was confident his guys could figure out its purpose.

As he walked back to sit on the log, one of his boots dragged against something half-covered with dirt and leaves. Wiping the small book clean revealed the dark leather-bound journal.

"This is the journal I gave Will," he shouted. Alvaro brought a flashlight. Under the circumstances, Alain gave himself permission to read it, and he began with the last entry. He flipped the pages and studied it again. Then he looked at the shelter. From what he'd read, there was every reason to believe he'd find answers there. He looked back at the inscription he'd written to Will, and the powerful irony was not lost on him. His parting gift to Will could be Will's parting give to him. He hoped he was wrong.

He was on the way up the steps when his phone vibrated.

"I'm hearing a lot of noise on the line," said Suzen.

"Sorry. It's windy up here." He had trouble hearing her, too, but he worried it had more to do with his aging ears than the phone connection.

"I understand, but you're going to want to hear this."

He moved behind a tree to get out of the wind. "Better?"

"Alain, the oddest thing just happened. The guys here managed to boot up part of the system. It was a monumental job, and it only ran for a few seconds before shutting down again, but it was long enough to spit out some data that has me completely confused. But I thought it might be of help to you."

"How so?"

"It shows that about six o'clock in the evening Will got to the campground. The coordinates match where you are standing."

"Six o'clock this evening? That's encouraging."

"Yes, and according to his itinerary, he was going to overnight there, so it makes sense. But it looks like he kept going, which is not particularly troubling. We've seen him hike at night before."

"So, you say he left this campsite?"

"Yes and no. It's hard to tell from the printout. I'm hoping you can help figure it out."

She explained she hadn't had time to analyze the report, but what had struck her as curious was that the readout showed his gear scattered around. Some was near the town of Harpers Ferry, and other things were still at the campsite. Until the system was online again, they wouldn't be certain which of his gear went where. "If I didn't know better, reading this I'd think he split up into several parts."

"Huh? I'm having trouble hearing. Did you say he split into pieces? What on earth do you mean?"

She spoke louder and read from the beginning of the read-out. She explained that some of his things left the area an hour and a half after Alain arrived. "And wait. Approximately a half hour later, more of his gear left. So, I guess that explains why I'm seeing stuff in Harpers Ferry. And something else left your spot very recently. The first thing was about thirty minutes ago."

That would have been about ten minutes before Alain arrived, and he was eager to know if she could tell him what direction the last bit went. Unfortunately, the output had degraded to the point of gibberish and no longer was readable. Unlike the other items that left earlier though, this last one didn't go back to the trail. According to the coordinates, this item went directly into the woods.

"See how this is confusing? Maybe he gave some of his things away, a t-shirt or two. We know he can be very generous."

"Yes, but that doesn't sound like something he'd do this time. He'd be more likely to give people cash than separate himself from his trackable gear." Alain asked her to break down the different tracks according to which piece of equipment went in which direction at what time.

"Sure. Give me a few minutes to assemble it, but I think everything I need to give you is right here. Oh, and something else. You know how we automatically calculate his speed? The person who took the first things must have been running. But how could Will run with all his gear?"

"I'm not sure the person running was Will."

Then he asked her to be more precise about the articles that remained, and she clarified there were still two items at the campsite: one near him and another about twenty yards away.

"Alvaro is checking out Will's tent, which is the one next to me." He gazed at the sleeping platform. "I'm about to look for the other thing."

When he reached the top of the steps, he gasped as he confronted his worst fears. A person covered in a dirty tarpaulin lay on the sleeping platform. In the dark, he could tell they were the right height to be his nephew.

"Will!" he whispered, hoping his nephew was only sleeping. When there was no response, Alain removed his night goggles to see more clearly. The body didn't react when he gave it a gentle rock, and his throat went dry. His fingers shook as he cautiously pulled back the tarp. What he saw next, he'd seen before, a neck contorted into an impossible and unnatural position. Will's stocking cap was on his head, which faced away.

"Alain, are you still there? I heard you calling Will's name. Is he there with you?"

"Um, I need a minute." He didn't peek under the cap. Instead, he pulled the tarp down further. The tattoo on the young man's bare torso took his breath away. His eyes welled up, and as he wiped away his tears, he quietly and respectfully pulled the tarp over the corpse again. Ignoring Suzen's desperate and repeated questions that came over speakerphone, he sat in silence and wept. Then, after emptying the deceased's pockets, he calmly walked down the steps and handed the contents and the daypack to Alvaro.

Suzen was still on the line when he picked it up. "I was so worried. What did you find?" she asked.

"A small backpack." He would tell her about the body later. For now, he would have to keep a lid on everything until he decided what information to release and when. He asked Suzen to remind him which way the last piece of gear went. His evening was just beginning.

Even with all the noise on the connection, she could detect the lump in his throat. "Alain, you don't sound good. Do you think Will is all right?"

"I'm not sure what's going on yet, Suzen, but someone got here before I did."

PART II

Chapter 10

Ask Me to Show You How to Poop in the Woods. The big, bold hand-written letters shouted from colorful poster paper. It was the first thing Marion saw when he entered the Hiker Lounge.

"A little late for that," he grumbled. He'd been on the trail over a week already, failing at every aspect of hiking and camping. Now they were telling him he was doing *that* wrong, too.

The Hiker Lounge occupied a large back room on the first floor of the gray stone Appalachian Trail Conservancy Visitor Center in Harpers Ferry. Because of its location - at the midway point in the famous trail that extended a little over two thousand miles from Maine to Georgia - the Hiker Lounge was a welcome and regular hangout for hikers going in both directions. Conveniently located on Washington Street, the town's main drag, it was a reliable place to rest up, meet other hikers, and catch the latest news.

Harpers Ferry and its National Historical Park sat at the confluence of the Shenandoah and Potomac rivers and three states: West Virginia, Virginia, and Maryland. Thanks in part to John Brown's famous raid on the local arsenal in 1859 and the poem that immortalized it by Stephen Vincent Benét, the town was a historic tourist attraction in its own right. Each year hundreds of thousands of visitors explored its quaint streets and shops, toured the battlefields, and took part in rafting.

One of the town's main attractions was the Visitor Center, the go-to place for everything non-hikers needed to learn about the trail. Maps and photos depicting the town's boundaries and lifestyle back when it was still part of Virginia lined the walls, along with trail memorabilia and portraits of its many famous visitors. Hikers and would-be hikers kept the docents busy with questions they hoped would help them decide whether or not to tackle the formidable trail.

The Gold Standard for hikers was membership in the Two Thousand Mile Club, which one earned by hiking the entire trail within a year. Volunteers were quick to define a year as three hundred and sixty-five days, and not a calendar year, hoping to make the monumental task sound more doable. Since many people weren't able to devote the several months it took to hike the entire trail at once, other options, called "alternative thru hikes," were developed over the years to break the trek into smaller chunks. In their spiels, they never tired of explaining the distinctions between "flip-flops," "leap frogs," and "wrap-arounds."

There had only been two people in the lounge for most of the afternoon: the guy on the couch and the guy at the terminal. When Marion sauntered in, they both looked up to give him the once-over. He was hard not to notice. Late-twenties or early thirties, tall and wiry with piercing deep blue eyes. Above him like a third eye was strapped a headlamp. He wore no hat and tamed his thick black hair in a man-bun. Most eye-catching, though, was the green backpack slung over one shoulder that stood out against his expensive black jacket.

He wasn't the first hiker to show up with high-end gear, just one of the few, because many hikers fell into two groups: students and temporary dropouts from society. They were folks of all ages who had tired of the daily grind and sought a more carefree lifestyle without responsibilities and many possessions. Many lived off modest savings, so someone with expensive gear like his attracted attention.

He made a beeline for the free coffee from the large thermos in the corner, squeezing by the hiker pecking away at the lounge's old computer. Maybe when the guy finished, he'd log in to find out if it was safe to leave the trail and go back home. He mechanically downed the first cup. Almost everything about the coffee was repugnant. It was thin and flavorless. At the moment, though, it was sustenance.

As he poured a refill, another sign on a wall caught his eye. One of the few hikers he talked to on the trail told him about the *Swap Box*, which turned out to be not a box but a teetering rack of plastic stackable bins. The guy told him it was basically a bunch of free stuff, and free was Marion's favorite price. What he hoped to find was fresh batteries for his headlamp, or better yet, a whole new headlamp. At present, he'd settle for a flashlight. It was tricky hiking the trail at night without one, and he didn't realize how fast his batteries would run down. In the city, he was considered a tough guy, but the woods at night gave him the creeps. If he had only listened to the salesman in the store and bought extras, he wouldn't have had to risk standing out in such a public place.

"Pretty slim pickings today, unless you wear a size seven shoe," boomed a voice from a clean-shaven hiker at the other end of the room. He wore a baseball cap with a black ponytail hanging out the back and slouched deep into the well-worn sofa. His stocking feet rested on the rustic wooden coffee table, and he looked very much at home.

The voice was right. The bin didn't look like it contained anything promising. Three pairs of worn smaller-sized sneakers spilled out over the top, and he needed size fourteen. Pawing through the castoffs, he spotted an opened package of water purification tablets sticking out beneath one sneaker. *Katadyn Micropur —effective against viruses, bacteria, cryptosporidium and Giardia.* Never in his life did he imagine he'd need protection against anything as disgusting as whatever those things were. But he did now. Further digging turned up a partial roll of toilet paper and a cheap plaid scarf. Still no batteries or even a flashlight, but not a bad find, considering he might have to go back out on the trail for at least another week. He hated the thought.

The idea behind the Swap Box was in the name. When you took something out, you put something back in. For a hiker, everything had weight or took up space, so southbound hikers would often leave their woolen caps and mittens for folks heading north, trading them for lighter clothing. He didn't see much of value today except the toilet paper, which everyone needed...even those who hadn't been properly shown how to poop in the woods.

"Yeah, not much here," he responded, attempting to disguise his New York accent. He was still rummaging through the box, not willing to give up hope.

"That's because the Swap Box is the first place everybody goes to when they come here. But most people need to dump stuff, so you never know what you'll find," returned the voice from the sofa.

The room was silent, except for the guy at the computer. By his keystrokes, it was easy to tell he was messaging someone. He'd type fast and follow it with a swat on the "Enter" key. Then he'd read the response before typing energetically again.

On the wall next to the computer terminal another hand-made sign advertised free long-distance calls from a dusty land-line telephone, courtesy of a local organization that sponsored the relic. The admonition of the block lettering was stern--*Call Your Mother.* Though hikers all had cell phones, signals on the trail were often nonexistent or spotty, and the challenge of keeping the phone's battery charged kept usage to a minimum.

Under the circumstances, Wi-Fi and a charging station might have been more practical for a company to sponsor.

Another swap system tower leaned against the wall next to the stack of bins. The flimsy shelves groaned under the weight of the books folks had donated.

"I just finished this," said the guy on the couch holding up a dog-eared copy of *The Dead of Winter*. "I got it from the shelf next to you. Most of those books are about hiking and botany and stuff, but this one is a pretty good horror story. Supposedly it takes place around here. Want to read it?"

"Yeah, maybe," Marion mumbled as he guzzled the rest of his coffee and refilled his cup a third time. Ignoring the talkative hiker at the other end of the room, he plopped down on a threadbare armchair and flipped through an album of photos he found on the adjacent table.

Most hikers passing through the Lounge at the Visitor Center had their picture taken and added to the vast collective that had accumulated through the decades. Lining another bookshelf were more binders full of hikers. They were organized and sorted chronologically. Judging from only the albums he could see, they dated back several decades. A color scheme explained by a chart on the wall identified the hikers by the direction they traveled. A green dot on the Polaroid photo indicated they headed southbound and red northbound. He was surprised by the recent entries. He didn't know Polaroid cameras still existed and wondered where people got the film. Someone added himself only a few days earlier. He was a handsome guy, too, with auburn hair. His photo bore a green dot.

As he sat staring into space, a rumbling sound from inside his black jacket broke the silence. It was louder than the only other sound in the room, the staccato cadence of the computer keyboard. Shortly his stomach let out another growl.

"Sounds like somebody's hungry," joked the hiker on the sofa.

Without turning to engage, the newcomer mumbled that he hadn't eaten in days.

"Yeah, I'm starving, too. Just not quite as obvious, I guess, ha ha." He pulled his feet off the table and walked over to extend a handshake. "Hey, friend, I don't know your name. They call me Tracker." His wide smile revealed a mouthful of crooked teeth. One gleamed silver.

"Um, I'm Bill," he lied.

"Bill? What do you mean? You have another name, and I think I know what it is! You are...you're...let me think now." Tracker's pauses made the newcomer anxious.

The guy knew he shouldn't have gone in the lounge, but he was desperate for a cup of coffee. Now he was afraid this guy, Tracker, recognized him. He started to sweat, and his eyes darted about looking for a way to get out of the place fast without attracting any more attention.

"You're Growler," said Tracker. "Get it? Growler, like the sound coming from your stomach. Yes, that's going to be your trail name. What do you think?"

Relieved, his broad shoulders relaxed, and he turned back around. "Yeah, okay, fine."

Tracker looked up at the large wall clock. "Hey, Growler, it's almost six. What do you say we grab some dinner?"

"Um, no. Don't think so. I'm a little short on dough."

Tracker laughed. "Your gear is top of the line. No wonder."

"It is? I didn't know. I traded some guy for it."

"Well, I don't know what he got out of the deal, but you definitely scored some nice gear. So then why are you broke, if you don't mind my asking?"

"Some creep stole my money one night on the trail while I was sleeping."

Tracker noticed he was wearing loafers and laughed again. "Did they steal your boots, too? If you're hiking north, you'll need to pick up a pair soon."

Growler was annoyed at having to carry on conversation. "Yeah, I am heading north, but I'm fine."

"Well, never mind. This is your lucky day, because I happen to be loaded at the moment, and tonight your dinner is on me."

Growler made a weak effort at turning down the offer, but Tracker insisted. A guy who owed him money finally came through and wired it to him earlier in the day, and he felt flush.

"Might as well share my good fortune. We're both starving, so it's a win-win. Besides, I can use the company. There's a joint up the street they say has pretty good food."

Growler grunted the obligatory empty promise to pay Tracker back one day, and they agreed to leave as soon as Tracker found his boots. With one final smack on the keyboard, the person at the computer pushed back from the desk and stood to leave.

"Oh, I forgot my manners," said Tracker. "Lana Lang, meet Growler. Growler, this is Lana Lang."

From the back, the oversize sweater and stocking cap gave Growler the impression the computer person was a guy, but now there was no question. He was a very attractive she.

"Lana Lang? You mean like in Superman?" He looked at Tracker, who returned a wink.

"Superboy," she corrected with a clipped response and ignoring his awkward attempt at a handshake.

As Tracker laced his boots, he asked Lana Lang if she had decided to join him or not.

"If you're still buying," she said on her way to the restroom. "But I'm only going because my boyfriend hasn't shown up yet."

When she was up the stairs and out of sight, Tracker made a fist pump. "She's been playing hard to get all afternoon, but I think she's into me. Anyway, I don't believe there is a boyfriend."

Growler wasn't interested in Tracker's love life, and he wandered back over to the Swap Box to make sure he got the toilet paper and the scarf before someone else. Since he wasn't planning to leave anything of his own in exchange, he took pains to hide what he was doing from Tracker. Pretending to select a book from the shelf with his left hand, his right easily slipped the toilet paper and other goodies into his pack. He wrapped the scarf around his neck to give the impression he'd worn it in.

"Hey, you still want to read this book, Growler?"

Startled, he dropped the box of water purification tablets, and they spilled out on the dirty carpet. Worried that Tracker had been watching, he scrambled to pick them up.

"You won't regret it. It's the best one on the rack today. It's a fast read, and it's really scary."

As Growler stood up, another huge poster stared at him from the wall. *Bears Want Your Food!* "Now that is scary."

As the three left the lounge and entered the main room on their way to the front door, a cheerful volunteer stopped them and asked if they'd like her to take their photos. "Everyone wants to be in the albums, you know, for posterity," she added with a touch of salesmanship.

"Mine's already in a binder," Tracker explained politely. She turned hopefully to the others. Growler shook his head and held his hand over his stomach, showing that he was too hungry to stop. Lana Lang dodged the volunteer's question and slipped out of the lounge ahead of the others.

The Visitor Center was uncharacteristically crowded for a late afternoon. People oblivious to closing time clogged the aisles between brochure racks and the display counters that burst with trail memorabilia. Souvenirs screamed *I Did a Flip-Flop on the Appalachian Trail* and *I Can't Believe I Hiked the Whole Thing!* One tourist clutched a fistful of free pamphlets, and two or three others engaged a docent in a spirited conversation.

It was a narrow fit through the aisles to get to the front door. They had to squeeze past a swivel rack of postcards and a rather disheveled older gentleman with jet black hair studying a display of sepia photographs on the wall next to the door. He was so engrossed that when Tracker accidentally bumped into him, the old man fell backward and collided into Growler, who lost his balance and wheeled around.

"Hey, watch where you're going!" Growler's outburst attracted the attention of the others in the room and startled the old man, who grabbed Lana Lang's wrist to right himself. She jerked her arm away.

"Forgive me. I meant no impertinence," he said. After hearing his apology, Lana Lang took his hand and helped him up.

"Wow. Did you get a whiff of him?" asked Tracker when the three were out of the building and on the sidewalk. "No wonder he fell down. I'm surprised he could stand at all."

The White Horse restaurant was a long walk down Washington Street, but Growler didn't mind adding those few blocks to his day for a free meal. Besides, it was nothing compared to the grueling time he'd spent hiking. To celebrate the good fortune of being treated to dinner, he determined to eat as much as he could get away with, without appearing too greedy. And without being recognized. He'd made it this far, but he couldn't afford to be reckless.

His strategy was to hike at night when nobody else was up, and sleep during the day, when everyone was out and about. He thought it was a brilliant idea, calculated to minimize the risk of being identified, but not thinking through how he was going to eat was a serious misjudgment that jeopardized the whole scheme. Growler was a New York City boy, and like many New Yorkers, he scarcely chose to leave. Armed with little knowledge of life in the outside world, he assumed that this park would be no different from the ones in the city. Where he lived, parks had concession stands.

An hour into his first day, he innocently asked two guys

hiking toward him how far it was to the next snack bar, and they burst out laughing at what they took as a joke. He was crushed by the rude awakening that hikers cooked their own food. Apparently, it was supposed to be part of the adventure, part of the fun. Having to exit the trail during the day to search for food in nearby towns -- often many miles away -- was not only an annoyance, it was dangerous. It interrupted his sleep patterns and made him grouchy. Since he had brought no cooking equipment, he had to rely on sandwiches and snacks, and he was tired of eating the same thing every day.

He learned that bumming food from other hikers was easier. He made up stories of how animals raided his supplies and left him in the unfortunate situation of being temporarily starving. He quickly developed a repertoire of practiced lies that produced some tasty meals, but at times, a hiker's generosity came with a cost. He remembered how one guy was a real talker and insisted on sharing their motivations for taking the plunge and hiking the trail. It was in that conversation that Growler learned his pat response, that his was a spur of the moment kind of decision, was an explanation that certainly sugar-coated what transpired.

His last racket ended badly and was bound to attract attention; Growler knew he needed to disappear fast. He came up with the solution as he raced from the scene in his stolen car. "Get away from it all!" shouted the billboard advertising the Appalachian Trail. Smiling hikers with sunshine beaming down on their faces announced an entrance twenty miles away. Vanishing into the woods and strolling the trail for a few weeks sounded easy and looked comfortable, maybe even fun, in an offbeat way. There was no time to consider the negatives, because he was in a big hurry. He didn't think he'd need much, either - a tent, a sleeping bag, and maybe a few other things. But Growler was unprepared in every way, like wearing loafers and never having enough toilet paper.

Relaxing on a real chair in a warm restaurant and ordering a free meal from an actual menu was such a gift, he deemed it worth the risk. Besides, if his current situation followed the patterns of his former jobs, he'd only need to hide another week.

Chapter 11

Growler was starving. From a few doors away, the aroma of sizzling steak told him they were close to something delicious, and he hoped it came from the restaurant Tracker picked. When they entered, he sensed something wrong. Country folks tended to eat early, and although it was six o'clock, there was only one other table of diners. He hoped it didn't mean the restaurant was no good.

"Welcome to the White Horse. My name is Lucky," said the middle-aged hostess with bleached blonde hair. She quickly sized up the group. "Hmm. Two smelly guys and a woman, all carrying backpacks. Y'all been hiking the trail?"

They nodded tentatively, hoping their hiker status and appearance wouldn't disqualify them from being served. Unfazed, she directed them to a tiny coatroom off to the left, where she said the management preferred they leave their backpacks and other gear, insisting that everything would be safe. Lucky ushered them to a darker room in back where she seated them at a long Early American-style table.

"We call this our Hiker Table. Most of you come here in ones and twos anyway, and we normally seat you together. I hope you don't mind sitting with a couple who arrived earlier."

Growler made a production of barging ahead of the others. He knocked into a chair as he commandeered the seat at the far end, which would allow him to keep his back to the room.

"You're acting nervous," teased Tracker. "Are you hiding from a woman?" Even Growler knew his laugh wasn't convincing.

Before he sat down, Tracker introduced himself to the couple already seated. The man was in his early thirties and sported multiple piercings in his lips and eyebrows. A huge, thick nose ring dangled behind two smaller ones, and two more-delicate rings poked through the sides of his nostrils. His long droopy earlobes sagged under the weight of shiny steel plugs an inch or so in diameter.

"I'm Hardware," he said self-consciously, as he struggled to pronounce the 'w.' "And dis is Moonbeam."

Lana Lang seemed transfixed, and Moonbeam noticed her staring. "Oh, these?" she asked, yanking playfully on his earlobes. "They're surgical steel tunnel gauges. He says everyone's got them in Berlin."

Lana Lang's face conveyed her nonchalance. "They look like napkin rings," she said.

"Aren't German guys dreamy? Hardware and I just met, and already he asked me to hike with him." Her voluminous hair was wild and multicolored, and she patted it constantly. When Lana Lang shifted her stare from Hardware's ear lobes to Moonbeam's hair, Moonbeam misinterpreted it as interest.

"Um, yes, my hair is hand-painted, if that's what you were wondering. I'd tell you who styled it, but you probably wouldn't recognize his name. Some people say it's my best feature… though it's not my newest, if you know what I mean." She jutted out her chest and searched Lana Lang's face for compliments that never came.

The awkward exchange ended when Lucky returned with a stack of plastic menus, which she placed in the center of the table. When Growler reached across the table to grab the first one, she gulped. "Wow, those are the biggest hands I've ever seen! I'll bet you could do a lot of damage with those suckers."

She wasn't the first person to notice, and since his hands weren't something he could easily hide, he learned long ago to ignore their comments. He wouldn't need to consult a menu anyway. As long as the portions were big, he didn't care what he ate. But he wondered how it would work. Could he order anything he wanted? It had been two days since he scavenged food from that guy at the campfire. With Tracker picking up the tab, tonight was his lucky night. Even their waitress was named Lucky, and he took it as a sign that his good fortune was only beginning.

In the meantime, as much as he hated conversations with strangers, he figured his benefactor would expect him to make an effort. Tracker seemed harmless; he might even be useful again. Besides, he guessed Lana Lang would get most of Tracker's attention, and maybe he'd be off the hook. Either way, he didn't care. After those dreary weeks on the trail, he deserved a relaxing and fun night out.

"Can I start you guys off with something from the bar?" Lucky's long hair whipped around her head like soft serve ice cream, and when she raised up her hands to write the order on her pad, she exposed a long phrase that scrolled around and up her left forearm. The swirl of the text matched her hairstyle and appeared to be a proverb or something in one of those popular and unreadable fonts made to look ancient.

Tracker was in a generous mood. "Is everybody down with beer? I'm buying,"

Moonbeam proclaimed that her first hike with Hardware called for something more festive, and Lucky brought her the White Horse version of a Cosmopolitan. Tracker announced he would order for Growler and Lana Lang, officially putting to rest any fears Growler may have had about ordering too much or too little. He asked for the biggest steaks in the house, with baked potatoes and sides of this and that. Growler was ecstatic.

"Lucky, these are my guests, so make sure they have whatever they want." Tracker requested a black bean burger for himself.

"Make that two." Moonbeam sensed a compatriot. "You're a vegetarian, too?"

"Not by choice," he answered, baring his crooked front teeth. "Why, are you?"

"Oh, yes," she said in a voice that rose and fell in a studied cadence. Frequently, she would pause and emit a humming sound between phrases, an affectation some people used to appear more thoughtful. "Eating animal flesh is, um, incompatible, hum, with being spiritual."

Lucky arrived with their drinks and another diner, the doddering older man from the Visitor Center. "Like I said, the peach rosé is my personal favorite," she bragged to him with a flirtatious twinkle. "But the rest of our wines are listed on the back of the menu."

He still reeked of alcohol as he teetered into the first available chair, and he was grinning ear to ear when he let out a loud hiccup. "I like to have a little glass of wine when I'm out with friends," he explained with a comic touch.

"Sir, didn't we just see you down the street at the Visitor Center?" asked Tracker.

The old man studied each person's face. "Oh, I don't think so." He made another hiccup, and he was apologizing, when a third hiccup cut the apology short. Then he broke into a big smile. "Say, now I remember. You're the ones I bumped into."

"No, I'm the one who is sorry, sir. I believe I knocked into you first," said Tracker. He motioned for the old man to slide down and join them, instigating muffled snickers as they shuffled their chairs to make room. Tracker then introduced everyone.

"Lana Lang, like in Superman?" the old man asked.

"No, Superboy. How come nobody knows this?"

"And you, young man, Tracker. It's nice to formally meet the man I bumped into."

"But we haven't met formally, sir. You haven't told us your name yet."

"I haven't?" The man looked surprised at the lapse and extended his hand. "Apple. The name is Mr. Apple."

"What a great trail name," snickered Moonbeam. "How did you get it?"

"I've loved apples since I was a child, and enough people on the trail caught me eating them, so someone gave me the name. Say, you look familiar. Have we met before?"

"Oh, I'm afraid not," she said, sharing a patronizing smile with the others. "That would be very, umm, unlikely. I've come from you know, hmm, *corporate*."

"Corporate? What do you mean, corporate?" asked Mr. Apple.

"I used to work for the GeoFibre company in New York. I was what you'd probably call an executive."

"Goodness. Well then, I guess we couldn't possibly have met, could we? My mistake."

Growler was ready for more beer, and Mr. Apple declined Lucky's recommended peach rosé and opted instead for a glass of Burgundy.

"Anything wrong with your beer, sweetie?" asked Lucky. "I see you haven't touched it."

Lana Lang cringed at the familiarity, and when she complained her beer was too cold, Mr. Apple leaned in. "I don't like mine cold, either," he confided. "And what do you want to bet that my Burgundy will come straight from the refrigerator?"

Recoiling from his boozy breath, Lana Lang quietly vacated the seat across from him and slid down to the next chair. Unfazed by her move, Mr. Apple continued studying the menu when Lucky arrived with two more hikers, both young men in their twenties. Gear Junkie, the livelier of the two, had the body type that hikers typically occupied -- fit and trim, but not particularly muscular. Along with his deep dark skin, Gear Junkie showed Asian features, and Growler guessed he was what people called Blasian, one of those new terms for kids from the increasing numbers of mixed-race parents. Streaming, by contrast, was pale and stockier. He was still removing his earbuds as he introduced himself to the others. Tracker assumed the role of host again and made the introductions to the rest of the table.

When he got around to presenting Hardware, Streaming did a double-take. "Oh, yeah. Hi, again. We passed each other on the trail the other night, but we didn't talk, did we? Nice to meet you."

"You know this guy?" Lana Lang asked Hardware.

"Um, no, I don't think so," Hardware said blushing. "Um, well, maybe I saw him once."

Streaming took the empty chair next to Lana Lang. "And you, ma'am," he said to her. "It's nice to see you again, too."

"Huh? Me? I've never seen you before in my life," she grunted. "I've been stuck here for days. And don't call me 'Ma'am.'"

Streaming shrugged off her rebuke and mumbled that he was positive he'd seen her earlier near one of the campsites. But he quickly changed the subject. "So, did you all come here because of the bears, too?"

"Bears? What bears?" Moonbeam hadn't heard the news, but she admitted being out of touch. "Since Hardware and I met, we've spent most of our time getting to know each other, if you know what I mean. We've hardly left our room," she giggled.

Streaming continued. "Well, some official-looking guy approached us with reports of a family of bears being aggressive to hikers in the area. He suggested we get off the trail and stay here for a few days. From his horror stories, we got the feeling it was more than a suggestion. I think he was trying to scare us into coming here, but he didn't have to." He winked at the others. "He had us at *bears*."

Tracker laughed. "Hey, Growler! Remember that poster in the Hiker Lounge about bears wanting people's food? Maybe they should change it to, *Bears Want MORE than Just Your Food!*"

Everyone was laughing at Tracker's joke when Lucky returned with Mr. Apple's glass of chilled red wine. He gave Lana Lang a private little smile, and he warmed the glass with both hands.

"So, how broke are you, Growler?" Tracker's question was so personal and abrupt, it surprised everyone.

Fearing Tracker would renege on the offer to pay for his dinner, Growler had to think fast. "Very broke. I told you, some asshole stole my money on the trail a while back."

"First bears, now robbers!" Moonbeam clutched her throat and asked Hardware if they should rethink hiking. She wanted to know what Growler was doing when they robbed him and a description of the thief. "Details. I want details."

"I only set the backpack down on the path for a few minutes while I walked into the woods to take a dump. It was in the middle of the day, too, and I--"

"Yech, stop!" she said, waving a hand under her nose.

"Hold on," said Tracker. "You told us earlier that you were sleeping when you got robbed. Anyway, it doesn't matter. The reason I asked was because I have a way we all can make some easy money." He told the table about a farmer he heard about near Harpers Ferry that paid hikers cash for odd jobs. You camped right on their property, and they usually provided meals. The owner of the curio shop in town sent hikers there all the time.

"I'm going," Tracker added. "After I pay for dinner tonight,

I'll be broke again. Anyway, it sounds like easy work, and I thought you might want to come along."

Gear Junkie and Streaming said they always needed money, and they suggested everyone hitch a ride together in the morning.

"Count me out," said Growler. It was out of the question that he would put himself out in the public that long. "There's got to be an easier way to score cash than manual labor for crap wages on some hick farm."

"What about you, Lana Lang? Want to join us for a couple days while you're waiting for your 'boyfriend?'" Tracker asked hopefully, putting the word boyfriend in air quotes.

"What's that supposed to mean? First, I wouldn't be caught dead working at some stupid farm! And second, my boyfriend is probably already around here somewhere looking for me."

Moonbeam also declined to work at the farm. "Hardware and I are going to take our chances on the trail. Besides, I don't have to work. I've got plenty of money for both of us."

"Aren't you worried that bears would be attracted by your smell?" joked Lana Lang.

"I know. Would you blame them? But I'm not worried. Hardware just now showed me he's carrying a gun."

"I've never met a hiker with a gun," said Tracker. He turned to Gear Junkie and Streaming. "You guys aren't packing, are you?" They shook their heads no.

Moonbeam continued. "We're leaving first thing in the morning, so naturally, we want to make it an early night. Don't we, honey?" she added with a wink. She took his hand and raised their arms as a testament to their bond.

"Oh, my god. You make me so jealous!" said Gear Junkie pointing at Hardware. Everyone looked confused except Moonbeam, who assumed Gear Junkie found her attractive. "No, no. I meant Hardware's watch. He's wearing an Epix, another thing I can't wait to get for myself. I looked online, but at the moment, they're way out of my league. The basic model starts around seven hundred bucks."

"Hey, Hardware. Can you show us your watch so we can see what he's talking about?" asked Tracker. Hardware pulled up his sleeve and briefly exposed the Epix, but he jerked his arm back when Tracker slid over for a better look.

"Sorry. I paid a lot for dis, and I don't like people touching it."

Mr. Apple changed the subject. "Gear Junkie, what an interesting name. Is gear the name of a drug young people take nowadays?" He punctuated his question with another hiccup.

"Nah. I've always been fascinated with gear — hiking equipment, tents, backpacks, all of it. I'm like the guy who knows everything about cars, but I get off on three-layer laminated fabrics and micro-seam allowance instead of transmissions."

Streaming verified he'd seen Gear Junkie in action. "He's a regular walking encyclopedia. Last night he went from person to person around the campfire, identifying what everyone was wearing, and he gave a rundown of all the features."

Lana Lang was unimpressed. "Big deal. Half the time the name's right on the front."

"To tell the truth, Mr. Apple, your shirt has me intrigued and stumped. I'm not up on vintage stuff."

"So, my clothes are vintage, huh?"

"I hope you don't think I meant any disrespect."

"Oh, none taken." His next hiccup was interrupted by a sudden and deafening screech. Everyone at the table plugged their ears and searched for the source. "Why are you all covering your ears?" asked Mr. Apple. "I don't hear anything."

Tracker leaned in close. "Sir, I wonder. Are you wearing hearing aids by any chance? I think maybe you need to adjust them."

"Why yes, I am. Oh, dear." Mr. Apple picked them out of his ears and fumbled with the volume control. "Sometimes I'm not sure these darn things are worth the effort. My hearing is perfect without them."

Gear Junkie pressed Mr. Apple for the brand of his shirt.

"I think it's Bernbaum, or something like that. You can take a look if you like." Mr. Apple pulled around the top of his shirt so Gear Junkie could read the label.

"Hmm. You're close. It's Berhnold. Never heard of it. Says it's made in Switzerland. No wonder I didn't recognize it."

"So, did you buy it there?" Moonbeam shared winks and stifled giggles with the others.

"Oh, yeah, sure," said Mr. Apple, sharing in the joke. "No, I think it came from Nordstrom. They may still carry them."

"What about my shirt?" asked Tracker. Even without a logo on the front, Gear Junkie easily pegged it as a house brand of a big box store.

"And a stinky one at that," interrupted Lucky as she set down the extra beers.

Tracker smiled at her but then took a whiff of his armpits to double check. Moonbeam made her humming sound again and commented that since becoming a vegetarian, her body no longer needed deodorant.

"Then what's that odor?" groused Lana Lang. "It smells like church or something."

Moonbeam thanked her for the compliment and informed the table that what Lana Lang smelled was patchouli. She admitted to being an expert on essential oils and would be happy to set any of them up as distributors. "Patchouli is my signature scent."

Mr. Apple flagged down Lucky and asked her to point him toward the restroom. As he wobbled to his feet, Tracker asked Gear Junkie to do Lana Lang next, but she wanted no part in the game and was quick to sideline any demonstration.

"Don't start with me," she snapped. "I like to wear my boyfriend's clothes, and I don't care what brand they are."

"Oh, no! Not the boyfriend again. You're breaking my heart," teased Tracker. He turned to Gear Junkie. "Well, at least the guy has good taste in sweaters."

"Growler's the one with the great stuff!" said Gear Junkie. "His Arc'teryx Beta AR is the best, but man are they expensive. It's going be my next jacket when I save up enough money." He guessed the Arc'teryx Altra 85 green backpack in the coat room was Growler's, too. "It's got composite construction suspension, and I've never run across one in absinthe green outside of a store before."

"I saw another hiker with the same pack a few days ago," said Streaming. "Not the exact one of course. Now that I think of it, the guy had a black jacket like Growler, too."

"That's saying a lot coming from Streaming," said Gear Junkie. "When we hiked together. he was always listening to music. And with earbuds in, I didn't think he was paying attention to anything else. I consider myself lucky I didn't fall off a cliff."

"Hey, not fair! Sometimes I listen to audiobooks." Everyone got a good laugh, and nobody bothered to ask how he got his trail name. "But you know, the guy who wore the gear like Growler's was cool. His name was Red Rover, and all his stuff was top of the line, not only the pack and the jacket. He even had an Epix watch like Hardware's."

"Which way was he headed?" asked Tracker. "Maybe I'll run into him."

"You might, but I doubt it. He's probably long gone by now."

"Speaking of going," said Mr. Apple. "I need to excuse myself to visit the facilities."

Lucky stopped him. Absent was her usual vivacity. She looked over her shoulder and made a quick survey of the room. Convinced that nobody was paying attention, she slid on an empty chair and told them she had horrible news to share. "You'll want to hear this, sir."

"What's the matter, Lucky?" Tracker asked. "You look like somebody died."

She made a fan with her menus, ostensibly to block the view from the remaining couple in the next dining room.

"Look, I don't want everybody and their brother getting nervous, so this is for your ears only." She put her hand to her chest and swallowed hard. "Darryl back in the kitchen has a police scanner on all the time, and he told me it's been going crazy with chatter about a body they just found in a shelter up on the trail. A dead body."

ALAIN WAS in the bathroom stall when he placed the call. "Suzen, you've got five minutes. I've got to get back to the table, or I should say Mr. Apple has to get back to the table."

"All right, I'll make it fast. The computer in the map room wasn't the only thing to catch a virus." She had worked into the night at the office, and as she explained what she learned to Alain, her body didn't understand whether she should be awake or asleep. It turned out that Dillon caught a case of food poisoning that knocked him out all week, and because he was the only one scheduled to work, his absence explained why no one picked up the phone when Alain called and why no one returned his voicemails.

"Who's this Dillon again?" asked Alain. "And remind me why he was the only one working?"

"I guess you forgot about the new server installation in our office downstairs. The changeover would take several days, and since the next Monday was a federal holiday and I would be out of the country anyway, I thought closing the Foundation and giving everyone six days off would be a nice employee bonus."

"So, no one was working at all during the week and the three-day weekend?"

"Not exactly. As I said, I arranged for him to make an appearance every day. Oh, and he's the new office manager we hired six months ago. If you would stop by more often, you'd--"

"Okay, let's recap," Alain interrupted, making a mental note to have Major M run a complete background check on Dillon. "Somehow our system dedicated to tracking Will got compromised, or sabotaged, as you said. At the same, time our office was unstaffed for an entire week, so no one knew the computer wasn't functioning. And all that happened while you were out of the country."

"Yes. That's about everything. What do you think it all means?"

"Well, I suppose it could be a huge coincidence, but my guess is that someone took elaborate measures to make sure we couldn't know Will's location."

"Do you think it's someone in the company?"

"I hope to find out. But it's clear that whoever was behind it wasn't working alone."

Suzen gasped. "I just remembered something! When I got back to the office the night you called, there was some opened candy on the counter. I thought it was strange because ordinarily the office was so tidy. Do you think someone sent it to make Dillon sick?"

"I think it's entirely possible."

He considered his predicament. He had nothing to work with, no description, no name, not even a gender. In his field, it was not uncommon to deal with an alias or two. Le Mauvais was a perfect example. If the papers hadn't given him that name, no one would have known what to call him, and Alain considered that since no one knew the real name of Le Mauvais' protégé either, or even the gender, they would be no easier to identify. He had to laugh. It wouldn't be easy. Since trail names were built into the culture, in this pool of suspects, literally every name was an alias.

But he had one thing in his favor. The assassin wouldn't have been able to disappear because when he gave the signal for the search operation to begin, his team swooped in fast. They entered the trail from multiple positions and rounded up every hiker they found within a hundred miles in either direction of Harpers Ferry. He knew he or she would be in the group he was assembling, and he was lucky there were so few.

Major M expedited the delivery of the device Alain found to the GeoFibre lab, and at first, the gadget mystified their experts. The connected earbuds led them to believe it was some sort of audio player and considering that they he found it on a trail popular with young people, it was a reasonable guess.

The flashing light that had caught Alain's attention was simple to explain. They used similar indicator lights on their own devices. It was the battery telling them it was running low, and it was a small matter to determine the proper voltage to power it up. They had several chargers with the proper plugs at hand. A sophisticated sensor at one end suggested it might detect beta particles or gamma rays, much like a Geiger counter. People were always searching beaches and other areas for artifacts, but this device didn't register metal, or anything else they put near it. While there was a consensus that the gadget measured something, they were at a loss to determine exactly what.

Because the shell was sealed, their investigation was delayed until an explosive's expert arrived for a consultation. When she dared cut open the casing and pull apart the halves, the scientists were astonished to find the inside was not at all mysterious. Components etched with tiny GeoFibre logos were clustered in the familiar arrangement of a proprietary device they used to track GeoFibre labels. It would be up to the team to determine exactly which label it tracked, and Alain de la Pomme to figure out why he found it discarded near a campfire.

Suzen choked. "I can't believe how well you're handling all this, Alain. I'm emotional enough from here, and I can't imagine what you must be feeling. Let me know how I can help."

"After a lifetime of finding myself in stressful predicaments, I've learned how to compartmentalize."

Thinking about how he'd conditioned himself to handle tough situations made him remember how new Suzen was to all this. "How are you, Suzen? Really?"

She took in a deep breath. "Honestly? I'm terrible. Will was my best friend. I haven't slept in days, and I can't remember the last time I showered or had a real meal. I'm grieving but I'm also pissed off. We *have* to catch this guy."

Suzen's fierce determination was a quality Alain always admired in her. But listening to how hard she was willing to work to catch his nephew's killer filled him with a surprising trust. He changed his mind and decided to tell her the rest of the truth.

"Look, there's something you should know. Will is alive. I've been sitting next to him at dinner, as a matter of fact. He's in disguise, too, and goes by Tracker now. But listen, I'm calling from a bathroom stall, and I've been away from the table for too long. We'll explain more later."

Chapter 12

"A dead body?" blurted Moonbeam.

Will contorted his face to match the horrified expressions of the rest of the group. Thanks to the acting classes his uncle insisted would come in handy one day, he convincingly pretended to be shocked.

"Hey," shushed Lucky. "Let's not start a panic. I'm sure the others will read about it in the morning paper."

The table was abuzz with questions. Was he a hiker and where did they find him? On her next trip to the table with more beer, Lucky brought an update from Darryl. She could now confirm they found the body at the Shady Pines campground, and that the victim was a male.

"Shady Pines? We were just there," said Streaming.

"So, they don't know who the poor guy is?" asked Lana Lang.

"If they do, they're not saying. And get a load of this. He was naked from the waist up. If that doesn't make you wonder."

Will and his uncle had a puzzle of their own. They wanted to know how two of the hikers at the table ended up wearing Will's clothing. While they figured it out, Will decided to have a little fun of his own. "It sure is puzzling. I didn't happen to run into the poor guy, but one of us must have. You all are hiking north, aren't you?"

Growler wanted no part of it. "Don't look at me. I've been going south, but I never ran into anyone."

"South? I swear you said you were going north," said Will. "Remember we talked about how you would need to wear something besides loafers?"

Growler claimed he heard it wrong and blamed the misunderstanding on their being too hungry to think straight. "Because I'm definitely heading south," he snorted.

"Do you think it could be Red Rover?" asked Streaming. "You know, the guy with Growler's gear. He fits the description. Last time I saw him, he was setting up his tent at Shady Pines. He said he'd changed his mind about stopping in Harpers Ferry and was hiking straight on through. I didn't ask why, but now I wish I had."

Moonbeam and Hardware said they had never met Red Rover, and when Lana Lang insisted that she'd never set eyes on him, either, Streaming looked confused.

"That makes no sense. I passed you and Hardware near that campground, late in the afternoon, about the same time Red Rover was there. I remember because you two were the only people still on the path."

Will remembered the couple passing him immediately after he got the alert -- Hardware wasn't easy to forget. He wondered why Lana Lang was trying so hard to pretend they weren't together, and he made a mental note to bring it up with his uncle.

"I just told you I've been stuck here all day." Lana Lang rolled her eyes and ignored him. Using a napkin, she wiped her silverware, glass and even the table under her plate. "This place is filthy," she complained.

Streaming persisted. "I remember Hardware's accent. Are you sure you don't remember me, we...?"

Lana Lang lost her patience. "How am I supposed to remember every stupid hiker who passes by?"

"Look, I'm not talking about every hiker."

Hardware stood up, interrupting the confrontation. "Does anyone know where dey keep da batrooms around here?"

Streaming pointed in the bar's direction, and Hardware asked if he would take him there. Curious about their conflicting stories, Will jumped up to join them, hoping he could learn something. He sensed that Hardware wanted to speak to Streaming in private, and to let them be alone together, Will used the restroom first. From inside, he pressed his ear to the door and heard Hardware whisper.

"Let's get dis clear. Of course, I remember you, but can we keep dat between us? I'm sure you can tell that Moonbeam is a little unstable. She won't vant to know dat I was hanging out wid another voman. I don't know vat she might do. And I don't vant Lana Lang's boyfriend to hear about it either, okay? Besides, nothing happened. It was a nice day and ve just vent for a little valk."

Will's mind reeled. Why would Hardware worry that Streaming would tell the others? Moonbeam's mental state was questionable, but he wasn't totally buying Hardware's excuse. She seemed more of a kook than someone dangerous. When Hardware was finished talking, Will ran back from the door and made appropriate noises in the bathroom. He flushed the toilet and ran the faucets. Then he made his way back to the table.

Ranger Cody had stopped by earlier, and Lucky was brimming with fresh details she didn't think he'd mind her sharing. They found a small daypack next to the body, and a tent pitched nearby, and they figured they both belonged to the deceased. Gear Junkie immediately wanted to know the brands.

Lucky had a puzzled expression. "Wouldn't knowing the contents of a backpack be more valuable than knowing the brand?"

"Oh, no. Brand names can tell a lot about the owner."

"Okay, then for what it's worth, the tent was high end, but the daypack was one of those cheap models."

Growler squirmed.

"Then I'd have to disagree with the authorities," Gear Junkie said. "I'd bet they belonged to two different people."

"Interesting," she said. "Oh, and the authorities first assumed it was a bear attack, but the coroner instantly ruled that out. Now, they're calling it a homicide."

"There's a killer on the trail?" gasped Moonbeam.

"Seems so. And apparently somebody with big, strong hands, because they say the guy's neck was broken." All eyes quietly turned to Growler.

"Hey! Come on. You can't think I had anything to do with killing anybody."

"Of course not, but whoever killed him must have known what they were doing and was strong like you because the victim was well over six feet. His pockets were empty, so naturally they suspect robbery. Still no name. At least if they know, they aren't saying."

Will kept a keen eye on the expressions around the table, as his uncle had instructed. "Gosh, who would want to rob a hiker? We never have money."

"They suspect another hiker. Not one of you, I hope," she said with a wink. "But I will give you a heads up. Tomorrow is going to be wild around here. The town will be crawling with cops."

"The trail already is," said the tallest of three new hikers who joined the table. He introduced himself as Tornado and his two friends, Einstein and Shoe Store, who seemed to recognize Growler. "Long time, no see."

"Huh? Oh, yeah." Growler shifted uncomfortably. "Uh, what exactly do you mean by crawling with cops?"

"When someone finds a dead body on the trail, believe me,

cops from everywhere come in. And if it goes anything like the last time, they'll want to check everyone's identification," said Lucky.

Tornado corrected himself and said, "Technically, they're rangers, not cops, who were sealing off sections of the trail." He continued that it was about the bears again, and they weren't letting anyone enter for a hundred miles in either direction, until the authorities made sure they no longer posed a threat.

"They were escorting us here for safekeeping."

"It feels more like we're prisoners," groused Lana Lang. "Did they tell you how long they're going to keep us?"

"Like I said, it being a murder and all, Ranger Cody told me they want to talk to all of you. And listen, I didn't mean to eavesdrop, but I overheard you mention working at Ridgefield Farm. It's near town, and if you left early enough in the morning, you could probably be there before the authorities show up."

Growler was the first to change his mind. "You know, tonight's been a lot of fun, and I'd like to hang out with you guys a few more days. I think I'll go to the farm with you after all, until things cool down."

"I'm going, too, but first I'm going to the police station," announced Streaming. "I can't say I knew Red Rover, but if he was the victim, I could at least identify the body." He looked at Hardware. "And I think you ought to tell them what you know, too."

Will jumped in before Hardware could answer. "Streaming, do you think you'd recognize Red Rover from a picture? Maybe there's one of him in the Hiker Lounge."

"Definitely."

Will could barely hold in his chuckle. At first, he thought to turn his face away, for fear Streaming might make the connection, but he thought of his uncle and didn't bother. Context was everything.

"I'd recognize him anywhere," said Streaming, staring Will in the face.

Streaming planned to stop by the police station first thing in the morning, if everyone was cool with that.

Growler grumbled. "Well, I hope you don't take too long. I'm really looking forward to farm life."

Will was astonished at how much alcohol Moonbeam consumed. The self-ascribed vegetarian spiritualist managed to toss back two Cosmopolitans while the rest of them were still working on their first beer. Later she polished off an entire bottle of peach rosé by herself and babbled on about how the drinks brought such clarity to her thoughts.

"Did I menshun I was in corporate?" she slobbered.

"Yes, you did, GeoFibre," said Mr. Apple.

"I started out as the receptionist, but as you can imagine, my job was much more important; I rose rapidly up the... what do you call it?"

"The executive ladder?" interjected Mr. Apple.

"Yes." She slurred her words and gestured wildly as she stumbled through her job description. "They must have recognized that I was the discrete type right away because most of what I did was top secret. You see, the owner was hiking the Appalachian Trail, and for some reason the people at the top didn't want anyone to know."

Will shuddered, fascinated by her revelation.

"I probably shouldn't be telling you either," she added with winks to everyone, "but I can't imagine it matters here in the middle of nowhere. Anyway, we're all hikers, too."

"William de la Pomme was hiking this trail?" asked Gear Junkie.

Will raised his eyebrows. Despite his relative celebrity status, he hadn't expected an average hiker to know his name, and he wondered why Gear Junkie was so familiar with him.

Moonbeam answered, "He still is, and I ought to know. My

job was to keep tabs on him. They have this huge map that shows where he is all the time, and I was the one they picked to report on his whereabouts."

"And how did you do that?" asked Alain.

"They gave me a special cellphone. Every day I called the same number and left a voice mail message of his exact location."

"Goodness, it sounds like something from a spy novel," Alain egged her on.

"I know, right? They said I couldn't let anyone see me enter the map room or make the call. Not even the lady who ran the place."

Knowing that no such job existed at GeoFibre, Will hoped that Moonbeam was just embellishing her job description, but if she had actually been hired by an outsider to keep track of him, he wanted to know more. "Wow, that is intense," he said. "If the lady who ran the place didn't know you were doing it, who hired you?"

Moonbeam took another slurp. "One day shumone who said he was at the highest level of the company called me. He told me he had to remain anonymoush, but that they had been watching me for a long time. Apparently, I impressed them with my work ethic, and he said quality employees like me are rare." She burped. "So, he picked me for a job he said was vital to the company. He swore me to secrecy. It was all very hush hush."

Gear Junkie was animated. "So where is Mr. de la Pomme now?"

"I quit a while ago, so I can't say exactly, but he should be about halfway through the trail about now."

"That would put him around here," said Alain.

"Well, you'll know him, when you see him. He's a real looker. Listen, I don't want you to think I'm self-centered or anything but Will –– I called him Will –– had kind of a thing for me. At least according to everyone in the office."

Will had never set eyes on her before, and he could hardly keep from laughing. "I'll bet he did," he said. "Why would you leave a neat job like that?"

"Well, I didn't need to work anyway, as I said. And you know, it was just time to move on."

Lucky came to refresh their glasses.

"Mr. Apple, I was wondering. Did you ever run into this Red Rover character?" asked Will. His uncle was unresponsive, and when Gear Junkie pointed out he had nodded off, Will gently elbowed the man in the ribs.

Alain sat up abruptly and pretended to be wide awake. "Heavens, my powers of observation clearly aren't what they used to be. I didn't even remember you from earlier this evening. And that was after literally knocking you over. So, I wouldn't know if I did."

He declined Lucky's offer of another glass of wine, and with a straight face, told the group he maintained a strict one-drink limit. What he said became a punch-line the rest of the evening, nearly always followed by a loud hiccup from someone in the group. He wobbled to his feet and announced it was considerably past his bedtime, and he still had some important things to do. He shook hands with each person at the table before he staggered out.

"I'm worried about him falling down," said Streaming, and he excused himself to escort the old man to the door.

"I'm worried, too," said Growler. "Worried he might stiff us."

"What do you care? You're not paying," said Lana Lang.

Almost immediately after Mr. Apple was out of earshot, Moonbeam started to poke fun at him. She wondered if he seriously thought he was fooling anybody with his cheap wig. "I'm a hair person, so I notice these things."

Gear Junkie came to Mr. Apple's defense. "So what if he had a goofy wig and he liked his wine?"

"Don't look at me," said Will. "I don't judge. With teeth like mine, I can hardly make fun of someone else's looks. Took a hockey stick in the mouth as a kid and always thought I'd get them fixed when I got the money. Then life happened."

"Talking about cheap wigs, what about Growler's ugly scarf?" Moonbeam's comment elicited a round of laughter. "It looks like something someone threw away."

Lucky brought them enough juicy tidbits to keep them drinking and talking for another hour, but when the pipeline of information finally dried up, Will asked for the check.

"I hope you kept them separate," said Gear Junkie. "With all the beers everyone ordered, it'll be a nightmare to figure out who got what."

"Oh, believe me, honey, I did." Lucky snapped her gum. "You're dealing with a professional."

Will jumped in. He knew covering the check would be no problem, but he wanted to ease the tension. "Look. Growler and Lana Lang are on my tab, and Mr. Apple only had a glass of wine and some French fries, so if he skipped out, how much could that be? I'll pay for him, too."

Moonbeam waved a hundred-dollar bill she produced from her bag. "That won't be necessary," she slurred. "This should more than enough to cover Hardware, the old man, and me." She ceremoniously slapped it on the pile of cash contributed by the others, knocking over a glass of water in the process. "Tell the waitress to keep the change."

"Nice to be in the company of rich people," said Gear Junkie. "I'm just a poor student."

"Yes, well, Hardware recently closed a big business deal, and I've been a lady of means for some time, so it's our pleasure."

"So, some of us are still meeting tomorrow at nine, right?" Will made eye contact with Gear Junkie, Streaming, and Growler. "At a joint called The Beanery, okay? It's the only place open at this end of town."

The others nodded in agreement.

Lucky appeared again with hot coffee, seven mugs, and apple pie for everyone. "I hope you left room for dessert."

"Hey, we're not paying for that," insisted Growler.

"You don't have to. This is courtesy of the older gentleman who left a while ago. He asked me to serve it at the end of the evening to make sure you all sobered up."

"That's a good one," said Will. "*He* wanted to sober *us* up."

"Yeah, funny, right? Oh, and he paid for everything, too. Even left me a big tip."

THE COMBINATION of low light and shadow was the most flattering that late afternoon and was ideal to take the snapshot. Sitting on the stone wall in front of the gray building, the young hiker struck a pose like a professional. One sneakered foot rested on the ground, and the other atop the wall, his right arm casually draped over his bent knee.

Though far from a professional photographer, in that split second, the volunteer caught Will in a fully relaxed and carefree moment. He was playfully twirling his wool stocking cap on one finger. Next to him on the wall sat his absinthe green backpack. A wide goofy smile exposing perfectly straight white teeth teetered on the verge of a laugh. Even the basic lens of the Polaroid camera loved him.

The sleeves of his sweater were pushed up and revealed something needing closer examination. "I wish I could see more detail," said Streaming.

Ranger Cody brought a magnifying glass and thanked him for coming in. "Identifying the hiker will be invaluable and will save us all a lot of time. And the other information you gave us might prove helpful, too. I'm glad I was here tonight. We're not usually working this late."

"I was going to stop by in the morning, but I saw your light on and took a chance. But we'll have to keep this quick. My friends are waiting for me at the restaurant."

Peering through the magnifying glass, Streaming leaned in closer, and the elaborate watch on the young man's tanned arm came into view.

Streaming tapped his finger lightly on the photograph with the green dot sticker.

"Yup, that's him, Red Rover."

"Are you sure?"

"Absolutely. I'd recognize him anywhere."

Chapter 13

Despite the gift of coffee, not everyone was sober. As she stood to leave, Moonbeam lost her balance and Will caught her.

"Oh, aren't you my knight in shining armor?" She looked deep into his face and batted her long lashes.

His heart thumped, scared she would recognize him, and he was relieved when she didn't.

He patiently walked her out of the White Horse and released her to the custody of a slightly less-inebriated Hardware. Leaning on each other for support, the couple staggered down the main street toward the town's hostel. Hikers dropped in late at night all the time, and the owners learned long ago to leave the door unlocked. It was easier to let people find beds by themselves and settle up with them the next morning.

Growler was inebriated and ready to turn in. Since he was drinking for free, he kept Lucky and the bartender busy, and Will never cut him off. He suspected Growler was determined to hide something, and he figured loosening him up with a few drinks might be just what they needed to get him talking. But aside from continuing to lie about inconsequential things, Will didn't learn anything new.

Gear Junkie, on the other hand, nursed two beers the entire evening and wasn't ready to turn in. Earlier that afternoon he checked into the Harpers Ferry campground, where he took a long hot shower. Since he'd already set up his tent, he planned to stay out as late as he wanted. The campground was just across the highway and only about a twenty-minute walk from town.

Will claimed not to have made any plans, but he had a suggestion. Up the hill above St. Peter's Catholic Church was the famous lookout, Jefferson Rock, and there were plenty of spots to roll out sleeping bags. "Any takers?"

"Is it far?" asked Growler.

"Nah. You must have passed by it on your way here."

"If I did, I never saw it. Anyway, the price is right. I'm in," he said.

"How about you, Lana Lang? Want to join us?" Will asked.

When she didn't answer, he turned around to see her staring at photos of dogs taped to a small storefront window. A sign begged for donations to keep the animals from being put down. *Save a dog. Only $50.* Lana Lang was tearing up. A woman emerged from inside and sadly shook her head. It was the last day for people to step up, and there were still animals they would have to euthanize.

"Will this take care of them all?" She handed the woman five one-hundred-dollar bills.

"Oh, yes. Bless you, bless you!" When the woman impulsively tried to give her a hug, Lana Lang squirmed away.

Will was touched at her display of kindness. He'd witnessed her tough exterior at dinner, but he sensed an appealing softer side. "That was awfully nice of you. What made you do that?"

"I've always had a thing for strays."

"You ought to come up to Jefferson Rock with us. We'd love to have you around. What do you say?"

"Rain check." She turned at the next corner, kept walking, and never looked back.

The four guys continued down Washington Street, past the tiny tourist shops and restaurants tucked into the stone buildings dating to the late 1700s. Soon Washington Street became High Street, and a few blocks later, they started up the steep steps toward the church, the midway point to Jefferson Rock. The blinking light from its cellphone tower spire shone brightly.

Growler took the lead.

"Hey, Growler?" Will asked. "I'm impressed that you know your way around. Have you been here before?"

"No. How could I? I'm going south, remember?"

"South, north, south, north," Gear Junkie said. "Are you still playing with us?"

Will added, "Yeah, Growler, come on. We don't really care that you're lying anymore. Just try to keep your story straight."

The evening of drinking was taking its toll on Growler. The steps to the church were relatively steep, but the climb wasn't normally challenging, yet he complained constantly and needed to stop at every landing to catch his breath. Finally, they saw the small wooden sign pointing to the bottom of the famous last flight of steps leading to the monument.

"Are you kidding me? Sixty-four more?" Growler was growing visibly irritable. Then he spotted the ruins of St. John's Episcopal, a church that burned down and was abandoned a century ago. "Hey, I'm done. I'm crashing here."

"No way! You've got to come up to the top at least for a few minutes. If I can do it, you can," said Gear Junkie.

Growler sighed dramatically before starting back up.

They started to climb again, and Gear Junkie counted the steps out loud. "Let's check if there really are sixty-four."

At the top, all four collapsed on a rock while they took in the panorama. Even in the dark, Jefferson Rock commanded a breathtaking view of the Shenandoah River.

"Streaming, are you sure you don't want to change your mind?" Will asked. "If you spent the night, you could wake up with this view at sunrise."

"I have no intention of seeing the sunrise anywhere," mumbled Streaming, reiterating his objective of sleeping in late at the hostel. After a long day of hiking mixed with the evening's alcohol, he nodded off. He lay down on one of the long flat boulders and announced he would rest for a few minutes before he left. In no time, he was asleep.

Gear Junkie decided to stick around a little while longer but said he still planned to spend the night at the campground.

"Too bad Lana Lang isn't here," said Will. "I bet she would have enjoyed the view."

"I don't get what you see in her," said Growler. "She's such a bitch." Streaming's heavy snoring overpowered their conversation, and Growler didn't wait for Will's reply. "That's another reason you don't want me up here with you. They say I snore."

"Well then, you're right. We wouldn't want you up here with us, either."

"Hey, Tracker. Do you know anything about this place?" asked Gear Junkie, patting the rock.

"A little." Will stood and assumed the role of tour guide. "Look, the Shenandoah and the Potomac rivers converge down there. Technically, it's called a confluence. They say Jefferson bragged to Europeans it was worth crossing the Atlantic just to see it, and for all his public relations, the country named it after him."

"Very interesting," Gear Junkie said, "but if this history lesson is going to continue much longer, I need a bathroom break." He strolled off into the woods, leaving Will and Growler alone.

"Hey, Growler, I'm still hungry. Want a candy bar?"

"Yeah, why not?"

Will made a show of fumbling around in a side pocket of his backpack. "Jeez. I can never find anything when I need it." He pulled out the thick wad of cash, as instructed by his uncle. "Oops," he said, face turning red. "I guess I should be more careful with this, huh?"

Growler's eyes fixed on the outward facing fifty-dollar bill, as Will suspected he would. "Where did you say you got all that dough?"

"An old friend finally paid me back," Will said shortly. "He wired it to me this morning."

"Oh, come on," Growler said. "I don't think you're giving me the whole story." He gave Will a poke in his chest. While it seemed like horseplay, Growler was drunk and overplayed both the joke and the jab. It caught Will off guard, and the push was enough to make him lose his balance. He lost his footing, too, and skidded sideways down the smooth flat rock.

"Holy crap!" he cried, as he slipped farther toward the edge.

Growler gave a half-hearted attempt to grab Will's arm, but his timing was off, and he was short by a foot. Will kept slipping closer and closer to the precipice, soon only seconds from sliding over the edge. Suddenly Gear Junkie appeared, and without hesitating, he flung himself into the air toward a vertical rock wall to the left of the precipice. His back slammed against the rock, and hanging on a tree root with one hand, he reached over to Will.

"Grab on!" he shouted. With only inches to spare before he would drop to his death, Will caught his hand. Gear Junkie pulled him away from the edge to the safety of the rock wall. They leaned on it for a while to catch their breaths.

Will was still in shock. "You saved my life, Gear Junkie. I'd have been a dead duck if you hadn't come back at that precise moment."

"Yeah, well, I couldn't let you fall and be the one to desecrate

Jefferson Rock for all eternity. It was bad enough they found one dead body on the Appalachian Trail already today."

Will tried hard not to think about how he escaped death twice.

"I didn't mean to push you so hard," said Growler in a feeble voice from the path. "It was an accident. I was just kidding around!"

The other two ignored him as they slowly crawled up the slippery rock to the safety of solid ground. Growler tried again to claim innocence, but he gave up when he finally figured they were giving him the cold shoulder. A minute later, he announced he was going down to the ruins. "I can take a hint," he said. "But I told you I was sorry."

No one responded, but they heard his loafers on the gravel as he went down the steps. Gear Junkie and Tracker sat together staring into the dark sky, when Will broke the silence. "Someday, when I'm on my feet, I'll find a way to pay you back for this."

"Hey, there's nothing to pay for. You would have done the same for me." Then he joked, "Besides, you have a tooth to fix first."

"Okay, but I'd like to try. Can you give me your contact info?"

Gear Junkie fished in his backpack and produced a card with his email address and cell number. "Yeah, look me up sometime if you feel like it. It would be fun."

Will glanced at the card before slipping it in his pocket. "Hey man, I'm sorry, but after all this excitement, I'm ready to crash."

"I don't blame you, but if you don't mind, I think I'll stick around for a while to make sure you're okay."

"Thanks, but I'll be all right as long as I stay away from the edge."

"And Growler," added Gear Junkie.

Will chuckled along as he rolled out his sleeping bag, but

inwardly he was alarmed. Growler's push might have been harmless…or maybe intentional. Someone attempted to kill him once already, after all. Will planned to go back down from the lookout soon, but he had one more show to put on.

"I still can't believe that goofy Mr. Apple bought us all dinner, can you? Thanks to him, I didn't have to use any of my own. It's all right here, see?" He unzipped a pocket of his backpack revealing the cash he'd shown Growler earlier. Though he personally trusted Gear Junkie, his uncle had been clear he should tempt both hikers by exposing the large sum and then gauge their reactions. "It's supposed to last me for the rest of my hike, but in case I go over another cliff, I want you to have it, okay?"

"What? I could never take your money."

Lying flat on his back, Will pretended to fall asleep, and Gear Junkie let him. Then Will mumbled again, "Even though I don't need the money anymore, I'm still going to get off the trail for a while and work at that farm. What about…?" He faked nodding off without finishing.

"What about me?" Gear Junkie stood and slung his bag over his shoulder. "Yeah, I'm definitely going there, too."

Chapter 14

Will never intended to fall asleep at Jefferson Rock. He faked dozing off to move things along. Streaming was still snoring loudly behind him, and Growler had already left. While he announced he was spending the night in the church ruins, it was just as likely that he went to the hostel to take advantage of the free bed. Gear Junkie promised to stick around for a while, but Will figured a few minutes pretending to sleep would be enough to convince him it was safe to leave. After the high-energy day and evening, the peaceful night was a welcome change for Will, and in the soothing quiet of the Appalachian wilderness, he allowed himself to drift. Before long, he fell into a deep sleep.

The sound of someone heading down the steps woke him. He was woozy at first, but when he snapped awake, he sat up and took a few panicked looks around. As far as he could tell, he was alone with Streaming. His friend was no longer snoring, likely because he'd moved to a more comfortable place wedged in a corner of two boulders. Will smiled knowing that Streaming would wake up to the incredible view after all.

Before Will took off down the trail, he checked his backpack. The money was gone, and his uncle was right again. It was as though Alain counted on it being stolen. Will had stubbornly trusted Gear Junkie, but now he had to face the harsh reality that he misjudged him. He tried to be objective, but he couldn't help feeling disappointed. This new wrinkle put Gear Junkie in a whole new light, and he was eager to learn how his uncle would view the incident.

Will checked his new Epix watch. While it wasn't the personal version that had been engineered for his original hike, it was still a high-end variety. It was creeping on the early hours of the morning, which meant he was late. He gathered up his things and headed down to Harpers Ferry, where he knew his uncle would be waiting.

SURVIVING an attempt on his life looked good on Will and Alain beamed, hoping the laptop's camera was accurately capturing Will's animated body as he leaped into his tale over the video chat with Suzen.

"So, there I stood with a dinner fork for a weapon to use against a psycho who was waving my pocket knife and holding a huge club. He scared me to death, but something inside made me think I had a chance. I jabbed at him, thinking I would frighten him with my fork, I guess. He just laughed and started swinging. I dodged the club the first few times, but then he lunged at me. You can't believe how scary it was to see someone trying to hurt me with my own knife. When I jumped back, he bashed my hand with his club and sent my fork sailing."

"What possessed you to think you could take him?" she asked.

"Nothing. I knew I was outmatched, but I'm not a quitter, so I gave it one final shot. I landed a sidekick to his knee, and he crumpled to the ground. It was the only thing I remembered from my one year of karate, but it worked like a charm. While he was down, I turned and ran."

The other guy yelped when his head landed near the hot coals. He jumped to his feet, wiping furiously at his scorched skin. He hadn't been down long enough for Will to make it to the woods, but he seemed determined to get revenge. Putting Will in his sights, he picked up the knife. His throwing arm still stung from the burn, and while he threw it hard, his control was off. The blade rotated and wobbled in the air on its way to Will.

"Man, it came at me fast. If it hadn't grazed the tree next to me and ricocheted off a different one, I'd have been a goner."

By the time it reached him, only the handle hit his head. He yelled as he went down, loud enough for the guy to hear. "My scream was authentic, because it really hurt like hell."

Once Will realized he was unharmed, he stayed flat on the ground to reassess the threat. The guy must have thought he was dead because he didn't come after him. He sat back down and appeared to be playing another game. Will was glad he wasn't the only one who found Pumpkin Menace addictive.

Will waited a while longer before standing up. Escaping was his top priority, and he wanted to be sure his assailant was distracted before he made his move. He inched his way to the large walnut tree that had taken the knife for him earlier. The tree trunk was wide enough to hide behind in case the guy looked over. He was careful to step mindfully, but in the dark he didn't see the large twig under the pile of leaves. It snapped loud under the weight of his boot. His assailant must have heard the noise because he got up and looked around. Will froze. But the guy sat down on his stump again and went back to his game.

Without a shirt, Will was cold, and he still had to find the rendezvous point in the dark. He was eager to finish his escape, but he waited behind the tree for another fifteen minutes before making his move.

Just then a hiker wearing a mask emerged from the path into

the clearing and crept to the campfire. Will stiffened and regulated his breathing. He couldn't afford to make a sound. The guy was now close enough to touch the man at the fire, and he wondered if the new guy was sneaking up to give a big scare to a friend.

"I knew I was wrong about that when I heard the horrible snap of the hiker's neck!"

"That was supposed to be you!" Suzen choked.

"I know. I had to work hard to keep from throwing up."

He watched in horror as the executioner picked up some of Will's things. The assassin didn't stay long, and Will heard the thud when the guy tossed something at the fire on his way back to the path. In a second, the killer ran off and disappeared into the woods. Everything had changed. There was a maniac loose on the trail, and now Will would have to watch and wait again before making a move.

The most important thing on his mind was to get to his rendezvous point. He was shivering. He had more clothes in his backpack, but it was still on the ground next to the dead man. If he waited a little longer, he could venture out into the clearing and grab it.

He was slipping carefully between trees when he heard the noise. His heart raced! Someone else had wandered into the campsite. He'd never seen the trail so busy this late at night before, and he wasn't taking any more chances. He bolted in the opposite direction of the noise.

Earlier that evening when he received the alert, Will followed the protocol to the letter, and after consulting with his map, he estimated hiking time to his rendezvous point at less than two hours. He spent the next few minutes establishing visual markers on the horizon that would serve as guides. But now in his hasty escape from the campsite, he'd run off in a different direction and changed his point of reference. In an unfamiliar and dense forest, shirtless and cold, he lacked the cues he'd been so careful to lay out. The intensity of his narrow escape left him anxious and confused, and panic-, as he wandered aimlessly through the woods. Finally, he was too cold and exhausted to continue. Choosing to wait until morning light to continue, he lay down and buried himself in leaves to fend off the chill.

Plan B used a different transmitter, and once Alain got within a quarter mile of Will, he was easy to find. "When I saw you lying there motionless, face up and without a shirt like the dead man at the shelter, it was déjà vu all over again," said Alain. "But knowing it was definitely you made it even more nerve-wracking. I held my breath for the second time while I nudged you to see if you were still alive."

"Some nudge," laughed Will. "My ribs still hurt."

"Maybe it was a bit hard, but you have to understand how desperate I was. But it couldn't have been that painful, because after you stopped groaning, the first thing you said was, 'Congratulations, Plan B must have worked.'"

Will was quick to tell him about the killing at the campfire, and Alain assured him that the team had already taken it away. "Then you told me I had to hurry because you had big plans for me."

"And I hope I didn't disappoint," teased Alain.

Suzen had another agenda, too, but whenever she tried to change the subject, Will brought the conversation back to the excitement that was still playing out in Harpers Ferry and to his uncle, who he referred to as amazing.

"You can't imagine how he can maneuver people into believing what he says, and how he gets them to volunteer information about themselves."

"Oh, I think I can," she said.

Ignoring her response, Will went on. "Here's what I mean. For the first two days, he wore this goofy wig. It didn't fit, and even the color was lame. To add to the effect, he put on this drunken act, which he said worked for him dozens of times before. Oh, and he's fearless, too. I mean he put himself all alone right in the middle of all those suspects, knowing one of them is trying to kill him!"

"Um, so did you," Suzen said.

Alain interrupted. "In case you're wondering, Suzen, it's in the de la Pomme blood. Nothing we can do about it."

"You're probably right, but I've got to get back to the main reason for this chat. I want to discuss what the medical team learned after they examined Will."

The coating of the large capsule was supposed to dissolve within a couple hours after he ingested it. Had it behaved properly, the tiny transmitter inside would have sent its signal earlier than it did, and it would have helped search and rescue teams locate him before the guy assaulted him. But a few things didn't perform as planned.

The capsule took longer to dissolve in his stomach than they calculated, and they already had a solution with a simple tweak to the gelatin formula.

"Probably because I over ate," said Will. "I had just restocked, and I hate wasting anything, so I cooked it all. Even after sharing some with the psycho, I ended up eating way too much."

"Yes, it delayed the release of the transmitter and the other devices until well after you set up camp. And sitting quietly at the fire didn't cause enough vibration to power up the generator. The scientists assumed you'd be more active."

"And I would have been, if I had known somebody was trying to kill me!"

The undigested food surrounded the device. The food itself wouldn't have impeded data transmission, but it created a different and unforeseen problem. It was the pasta. Will ate so much that the food cushioned the generator from the vibrations.

"Well, that's all good news," said Will.

"Why?" asked Suzen.

"Because those are problems we can easily solve for the next time."

"The next time? I don't like the sound of that," she said as she signed off.

Alone in the room with Will, Alain poured them each another glass of wine. He was proud of his nephew's courage and overjoyed at the way he assumed the identity of Tracker and infiltrated the group of hikers so convincingly. But he was not all smiles.

He switched to French. "I didn't want to say this in front of Suzen, but François, you really had me scared for a while up there at the campsite. I hadn't gotten your confirmation signal, and I didn't know if you'd received the alert or not. I hoped and prayed I wasn't too late."

Alain's heart gave a little squeeze as he looked over his nephew, healthy and safe. He always hoped Will would get mixed up in his crazy life somehow, but he never wanted to put his nephew's life in danger. Though Will was a man now, he couldn't help but see him as the brave little toddler who would waddle around his château, looking for things to meddle with.

In a rare moment of vulnerability, he confessed, "I'm so glad you're okay, François. I don't know what I would do if anything horrible had happened to you. Losing your father was hard enough. I couldn't handle losing you, too."

Will's eyes clouded over at the mention of his father, but a smile came. "I miss my parents all the time, but you were a damn good substitute, Alain. I'm lucky to have you."

Alain patted his shoulder warmly but transitioned back to the topic at hand. "You know, under that cover, the body looked just like you, and I could totally understand how from the back and in the dark, the killer could have mistaken him for you. It was an eerie feeling."

They sipped their wine quietly and let their feelings sink in.

Alain attempted to break the tension, "I'm a little annoyed with you for making me wear that hearing aid. It was a great addition to my disguise but hit a little too close to home."

"What do you mean?"

Alain shrugged. "It reminded me I'm getting older. Sometimes I think I really do need one, but I wouldn't be caught dead wearing a bulky monstrosity like the one you made me wear for my costume."

"Oh, I'm sure we can find you something high-tech and unobtrusive." Then Will added, "You know I was just thinking. Why didn't the killer leave the scene of the crime as soon as he murdered the guy?"

"How could he? With all our men and drones and everything, it would have been very difficult," said Alain. "I'm afraid last night we ate supper with our killer."

Chapter 15

While Will got into his position for the next step of the plan, Alain called Suzen to coordinate their notes and review the list of suspects.

"At least now I know what you meant when you said you were 'in the field,'" Suzen told him. "You guys needed to put together your disguises, and then you had a whole restaurant to set up."

Making the White Horse look open for business again wasn't hard. When it folded six months earlier, the owners abandoned the building, but they left the fixtures and kitchen equipment behind. Major M provided the manpower to get it cleaned and Alain only needed a staff of one to give the illusion it was a working restaurant. Will cleverly talked most everyone into ordering the same entrée, making it easy to bring in the meals from a nearby diner.

"I can picture a cook named Darryl back in the kitchen listening to the police scanner," she laughed.

"That was Lucky's idea. Leaking news a little at a time created drama, and wanting more, the group stayed longer. Will was brilliant, too. I'm glad his mother made him take some acting classes."

Alain went on. "The killer didn't stand out, but we learned a lot." By now he was convinced that any description Major M might have provided would not have been much help. The men in the group were close to the same age, size, and build, and they all had long hair, which was irrelevant. Hair was the first feature criminals changed.

His staff was already at work transcribing the dinner conversation he secretly recorded, and they would be busy working up profiles of each hiker from both what they said and their reactions to others. Major had offered the use of his new facial recognition AI, which purported to interpret emotions and suggest intentions. Though Alain knew the mind-boggling technology often produced stunningly accurate conclusions, he declined. After decades of experience, he was more confident using his own intuition. Besides, he didn't have the luxury of waiting for someone else to arrive at the same conclusions.

"Will and I were shocked to learn that someone at GeoFibre was giving away secrets," said Suzen. "We've got to figure out who this Moonbeam character is."

While Moonbeam was obviously her trail name and not going to be in the employee files, she said she only recently quit the company, which would narrow down the search. Thanks to the peach rosé, she let slip where she was from, which would help immensely.

"There can't be many employees in the GeoFibre HR files from Poughkeepsie," she said, and she ordered a search right away. The company had grown significantly since the days when she knew every employee by name, still, she recalled no one as voluptuous as Alain described.

"Oh, I doubt she looked anything like she does now. In fact, she bragged that her newest feature was her breasts. Tornado, who I know has a great deal of experience in this matte, insists her boobs looked fake. He guessed she more than likely had a few other nips and tucks done, as well."

Growler, on the other hand, was the textbook definition of shady. They'd caught him telling lies several times. They were white ones mostly, dealing with seemingly inconsequential things, like which direction he was heading, and the circumstances under which someone allegedly stole his money and food. Alain couldn't figure out why he bothered. His hands were certainly capable of making the signature executions, and he had Will's coat and backpack. Lucky verified that with a quick trip to the coatroom. While possessing the gear didn't prove he killed for it, the information put him on Alain's short list.

"Why are we calling it a short list?" asked Suzen. "Everyone seems to be on it. Do you think the killer could still be on the trail, and we missed him?"

"I can't imagine how. Our drone coordinator reported they thoroughly covered every square meter of the target area. It's hard to conceive anyone sneaking past us. No, as I told Will, I believe we've met him or her and just don't know who it is yet."

He laughed and suggested she might enjoy hearing about the unexpected love triangle he discovered. "I almost lost it when I learned that Hardware was not only having a relationship with Moonbeam but also with Lana Lang. To keep my jaw from dropping, I had to keep making those crazy hiccups."

"Good grief! Can you think all three of them are connected in some way to your assassin?"

"Well, that's just it. I had to stop and remind myself that usually the simplest explanation is the best one."

"And what's that?"

"That Hardware is a serious ladies man, and what we have going on here is a good old-fashioned *ménage à trois!*"

She laughed along with him. "One second. Here, I printed out everything we have on Esther Blankenship, a.k.a Moonbeam." He heard her shuffling papers. "No wonder I didn't recognize her. She definitely worked here, but she lied about her title. We hired her as a file clerk in the billing department. A couple months ago, she took all her personal days off and said she needed to care for her sick grandmother. Our policy is not to challenge a request of that type, so we let her. Turned out that was a lie, too. Anyway, she left a Plain Jane and came back a couple weeks later as a Triple D. She stayed on for a while more and then quit just last week."

"Are you sure she only worked in billing? I could swear I saw her somewhere else."

"Well, it looks like she started out in bookkeeping, but the last five or six months she filled in upstairs with us at the Foundation, running the office kitchen."

"Now I remember," said Alain. "She made me hot chocolate once."

"Her record contains complaints from another employee about her making unwanted sexual advances. Looks like she quit before we had to terminate her."

"Anything else?"

"Yeah. Now I remember. This was the woman who bragged to some of the staff on her way out the door that she didn't need the job, anyway. The grandmother she allegedly cared for died and left her a hundred thousand dollars."

"Thanks, Suzen. The bequest explains how she could afford a breast augmentation. I don't know what any of this has to do with the assassin who's after Will, but I'll have someone dig deeper."

"And here I thought Growler was our guy, with his record and everything else. Now, I'm not so sure," Suzen added.

"Didn't Lucky pull prints from everyone?"

"Everyone except Lana Lang, but I'm not surprised. She's a real clean freak. I caught her wiping off her glasses and silverware. We'll try to get some tomorrow. But what makes her especially suspicious is that she's been wearing Will's sweater."

Alain expected the report from the FBI lab down the road in Martinsburg to show at least one hiker with a record. As a foreigner, Hardware was an easy catch. Customs and Immigration got his basic information when he entered the United States. Though they reported his flight originated in Switzerland, Alain was right about his accent. Hardware carried a Bosnian passport. But his file came back clean, except for a five-year-old DUI. Still, Alain thought it fishy that Hardware made such a lame excuse to keep Will from looking at his watch.

"Will's request to see it up close didn't play out because Lucky interrupted him. I'm going to keep trying to determine if it's Will's. And you're right about Growler. He's a prosecutor's dream, with a rap sheet a mile long. On the face of it he'd be the first one the cops would likely want to run in. But I honestly wonder if he's smart enough to be an accomplice to the crack assassin who eluded Interpol and me and every other agency for years." Alain sighed. "I guess it's possible he's a good actor."

Tornado, the team's newest member had been embedded in the trail as a hiker. He was still trying to mine information from Shoe Store and Einstein, the two young men he'd pulled off the trail and befriended, but he told Alain not to expect much. After running Gear Junkie's real name from the card he gave Will, they'd learned that his story checked out. While Streaming hadn't given Alain a reason to suspect him, he was traveling solo, and the agency had proved that lone wolves make viable suspects. On the Appalachian Trail, though, it was a fact that over eighty percent hiked alone, at least until they met people and paired off. The last one on the list was Dillon, whose arrest record was clean, even if his sexual habits were reportedly kinky.

Prints or no prints, Lana Lang remained a mystery. She claimed to be waiting for a boyfriend, but aside from showing a softer side when she made that generous donation to the animal shelter, she'd been so unpleasant at the restaurant, Alain couldn't picture her with a partner. Apart from keeping her relationship with Hardware from everyone, Lana Lang didn't strike Alain as dishonest.

"The boyfriend is the wild card. We need to double down and find out more about him."

"But how can we hope to locate someone without a name or a face? I mean, how would you begin to think outside the box?"

"Suzen, now that you are working with me on this project, it's time you learned that my way of problem-solving is not to think inside or outside. It's not having a box at all."

Alain felt things would come together soon. The presence of law enforcement sniffing around would put the killer on edge, and a nervous person is easy to pick out. But there was someone else he thought could provide valuable information. When Streaming confirmed Red Rover's identity in the photograph, it verified what Alain already suspected. From the time Streaming said he saw Red Rover to when he showed up at the White Horse, given average hiking speed, Alain calculated Streaming would have crossed paths with the killer. In the morning, he'd find time to speak to him alone.

Before hanging up with Suzen, he left her with one last tidbit. "I need you to play a couple parts for a video we'll need. I made arrangements with the GeoFibre studio and sent you the script. If you thought the restaurant scene tonight was elaborate, wait until you see what we've got in store tomorrow afternoon. We're really going to crank things up."

Chapter 16

an You Help Us Identify the Victim? The posters were taped to the front door, on the windows, and one was even slapped on the front of the cash register of The Beanery that morning. Somebody had done a lot of work on a Saturday night to get them printed and put up, but when there's a dead body found on the Appalachian Trail, many people get involved — federal, state, and local people.

The trail originally had its own rangers, but in 1968, Congress officially designated it a National Scenic Trail, and things started to get complicated. With its new federal protection, the National Park Service and the USDA Forest Service also had jurisdiction. In some places, the trail ran over non-federal government lands, making it more than a little confusing to know exactly what kind of infraction triggered which legal entity. In a case where there was a dead body, determining which of these entities had jurisdiction depended on exactly where they found the body, and if there was foul play. The Department of State would get involved if the deceased was a foreigner, and at the slightest suggestion of terrorism, the Department of Homeland Security would trump them all.

That morning, though, the onslaught of any authority had

yet to arrive. For now, it was only the flyers, and they were the work of Ranger Cody. The flyer didn't contain many details, only a description of a thirty-year-old male, about six foot two, with auburn hair. Along with the text was a photo of an empty shelter identified as Shady Pines. The three-sided shelter would look familiar enough to the locals. You could find structures like it up and down the trail like rest stops on a toll road.

Large print on the poster urged anyone who knew anything at all about the identity of the man to "contact the authorities immediately," although it was unclear which authorities.

Alain de la Pomme made a point of arriving early, and he sipped his coffee alone in a corner booth. Will designated The Beanery as the meeting place for everyone going to work at the farm. The plan had been for them to hitch a ride, and who showed up would tell Alain a lot.

Gear Junkie arrived first, and he commandeered a table in the center of the room. The few couples already seated were buzzing about the poster and the tragedy that happened only a few miles away. One woman blamed it on a drug overdose, and her husband attributed it to the lack of a military draft that spawned a generation of ne'er-do-wells.

"From what I heard, they're calling it a homicide," the waitress named Becky told Gear Junkie as she poured his coffee. "Somebody snapped the poor guy's neck, you know...execution style." She pantomimed the act with her hands and accompanied it with the glottal sound she thought described the action. *Gacke!*

"Why in the world would anyone want to kill a hiker?" asked Gear Junkie. "If I only had a newspaper."

He soon got his wish. Each time the door to The Beanery opened, a tiny little bell at the top tinkled before it slapped against the glass pane. This time, the tinkle was followed by a thud, made when the small bundle of newspapers hit the floor just inside the door. It was loud enough to cause the young cashier to look up from her texting. With a shrug and a sigh, she reluctantly set down her phone and shuffled across the room. Gear Junkie beat her to it.

"Here, let me do that," he said, offering to pick up the bundle. The headline blared out in giant type. "Oh, my god, people! You've got to see this!"

The not-very-noisy room quickly became silent as he read aloud, "Tech Billionaire Believed Missing on Appalachian Trail."

"Do you think he's the dead guy in the poster?" asked the woman at the next table.

"The article only says he's missing, not that he's dead," said Gear Junkie. "Anyway, jeez, I hope not. I mean, this guy is one of my heroes."

"Who is he?" asked Alain from across the room. He was disguised as Mr. Apple and was trying to gauge just how much Gear Junkie knew about Will.

"William François Chillon de la Pomme is a tech superstar. You've probably heard about one of his inventions, The Doodad. You know, that thing that keeps track of your stuff. It was really innovative when he came out with it. These days there are lots of knockoffs and you can get them everywhere."

"I think my nephew has one of those hooked to his car keys," said Alain, smiling at his genius idea of selling a separate line of knockoffs.

"Land sakes," said the woman. "You can get to be a billionaire by inventing something like that?"

"Yes, but I heard it was a little more complicated than it sounds," said Alain from his booth.

Gear Junkie summarized the rest of the article, including that GeoFibre had been monitoring Will's location as he hiked the trail through the labels sewn in his clothes. Becky asked the question on everyone's lips. *How in the world could the guy who invented something that finds lost objects end up being lost himself?* It was inconceivable.

"I know. It makes no sense. GeoFibre's tracking system has the reputation of being bulletproof. There had to be something more than a glitch in the system to allow this to happen," said Gear Junkie.

"How do you come to know so much about the guy?" asked Alain.

"These days everyone in business school studies him. I heard him speak once when I was in Thailand…"

Alain choked on his coffee.

"…on a fellowship." Gear Junkie continued reading about an agreement William had with his staff. If, for any reason, they lost track of him for seven days in a row, they were supposed to call in the troops. Literally. "That means he has been missing for at least a week!"

"Maybe it's because of the bad signal up there," offered Becky. "We can barely get service at our house, and we live right here in town."

The newspapers sold out quickly, and people were so engrossed in the story, they finished eating in silence. Even Becky respected their need for quiet and refilled their cups on tiptoe. Gear Junkie remained confused. "The article still doesn't explain how his company could lose track of him."

Becky turned on the television mounted on the wall. "Let's see if someone on the news has the answer."

At exactly nine a.m., the tiny bell tinkled again when Lana Lang made her entrance. Wearing a scowl, she plopped down at Gear Junkie's table and glared up at the wall clock. "Where's everyone? I thought we were meeting at nine."

Gear Junkie gazed over the top of his newspaper. "Don't ask me. And what are you doing here anyway? Last night you told us working on a farm was the last thing you would do."

She shrugged. "Yeah, well, the longer I thought about it, the more I decided I'd be safer out there. A single woman can't be too careful, you know, and what with a killer running around."

"But what about your boyfriend?"

"Oh yeah. He'll just have to wait for a couple of days, I guess, won't he?"

"Where are the others?" asked Gear Junkie.

"How would I know? I ditched you all as soon as I could last night. I stayed at that filthy hostel, but at least I got a private room. Those losers are probably still sleeping it off."

"I wouldn't know. I stayed at the campground up across the highway. Streaming said something about bunking at the hostel, so I guess you and the others were in the same place. Still, I'm surprised Streaming hasn't shown up yet." Then he remembered. "Wait, of course! He said he was going to the police first, remember? We agreed we'd wait for him."

"News flash!" Lana Lang threw her hands in the air. "He never went to the cops. Last night he made such a big deal about me going to the station, I went there this morning, not that I could add anything that would help with their investigation. Anyway, it was a total waste of my time since he never showed up."

"Ouch! Somebody's in a bad mood this morning," joked Gear Junkie.

"Yeah, I didn't sleep very well, either. Anyway, I'm not waiting around much longer. It's supposed to rain soon."

Alain was intrigued she showed up at all, given how adamant she'd been about not going. Still, he couldn't fault her reasoning. Hiking as a single woman with a murderer possibly still in the area was unsettling, though he knew the assassin wouldn't be interested in randomly attacking innocent hikers. After trailing her roundabout route to the hostel, he knew she had been truthful about where she stayed. This morning's lie about going to the police confused him, and he searched for a motive. And there was something else a little off about her. He hoped he could put his finger on it sooner rather than later.

Lana Lang stopped the waitress and ordered a black coffee. "Separate checks," she barked.

"Sure thing, sweetie." Becky rolled her eyes for the benefit of the cashier, who happened to be looking up from her texting. In solidarity, she returned Becky's eye roll with one of her own.

"Five more minutes, and I'm splitting. It's going to be a zoo around here." Lana Lang picked up the flyer from their table and registered her disapproval. "This is so stupid. How is anyone supposed to know who this guy is without a picture of him?"

She was still studying the flyer when Becky turned up the volume on the television. She hit the button too many times, and the blaring took everyone by surprise. Annoyed, Lana Lang covered her ears and scrunched her face as Becky struggled to find the right button to turn it down. When the sound returned to normal, Lana Lang glanced up and looked surprised to see William de la Pomme's name captioned below the face staring from the screen. She stared at the newspaper's front page for a second and looked back to the television.

"Oh, I guess you didn't hear about the rich guy who's apparently missing on the trail," said Gear Junkie. "We've been wondering if he's the dead guy on this flyer." He slid the front section of the thin newspaper across the table. "Have you ever heard of him?"

"I thought we were leaving," she snapped.

Becky said, "If you thought it was going to be crazy around here before, wait until you see all the extra cops they'll put on this case now. We're really going to be slammed today. Glad I'm working a double shift. I'll finally make some good tips."

Gear Junkie convinced Lana Lang to give the others five more minutes, reminding her it had been a late night for everyone. Her first coffee came. Then the second. When Gear Junkie left to use the restroom, Alain watched her scoop up the flyer and newspaper and stuff them in her backpack. He also noted she constantly looked down at her lap, presumably checking the time and expecting it to change radically, minute to minute.

The television talking head announced breaking news of a press briefing in progress and Alain smiled when Suzen's familiar face filled the screen. She verified that William de la Pomme had been hiking the Appalachian Trail, and while everything had been going according to plan, they lost track of him the previous Sunday when he stopped for the night approximately nine miles south of Harpers Ferry. He was to set up camp and continue hiking the next morning. In fact, he was ahead of schedule.

A reporter shot up his hand. "It's been widely reported Mr. de la Pomme was a stickler for procedures. If that's the case, how is it possible you could lose track of him?"

Suzen interrupted. "Let's get something straight right away. Mr. de la Pomme *is still* a stickler for procedures. Not *was*. Until we find out something to the contrary, we consider him very much alive."

"I stand corrected," said the reporter. He rephrased his question. "But, how could you lose track of him? Did somebody get sloppy?"

Sloppy was not a word in the vocabulary at GeoFibre, Suzen insisted, as she continued to spin her story. No, instead, she explained a chain of unusual events that allowed a lapse in monitoring. They were still reviewing their logs to find out exactly what went wrong. The reporter asked for a clarification.

"Let's call it a glitch," she said, and she offered to take one final question.

It was the delicate question everyone wanted answered. "Is there any reason to connect his disappearance with the deceased man they recently found at a shelter?"

"No, none whatsoever."

Lana Lang scoffed, "You'd think with all their money, someone in that family would

come here to look for him."

It was almost as though Suzen anticipated Lana Lang's question. "A member of his own family is heading up an extensive search, and he will be there in several days." She thanked everyone for coming and concluded the briefing.

Lana Lang raised her hand like a reporter with a question. "Hey! Can we go now? Who gives a crap about some idiot French guy?"

"He's not French. He's Swiss," Alain corrected.

"Like I said, who cares?" she mumbled back without looking. "Sounds like he's dead now, anyway."

All eyes turned to the front door when the bell tinkled the arrival of someone new. Wearing a pair of cheap dark glasses, Growler loomed large in the doorway.

"Nice shades. Is it your latest disguise to hide from all those women chasing you?" teased Gear Junkie.

Lana Lang jumped in. "And what happened to that ugly scarf you were wearing last night?"

"What are you doing here?" Growler asked. She ignored his question and called for a refill.

Growler looked around the room. "I wonder if they have any aspirin around here. I didn't sleep very well."

"I can't imagine why. Those church ruins didn't look comfortable," said Gear Junkie. "I'm surprised you didn't go straight to the hostel last night. With the rangers paying for everybody's rooms, it's hard to believe you didn't take them up on the offer."

Growler froze. "Wait a minute. I could have had a free room all this time?"

"You didn't know?" Gear Junkie asked. "They told everyone on the trail."

"Well, they didn't tell me."

Alain knew it would have been difficult not to get the message to Growler. Their network of rangers was setup systematically to catch people hiking north or south, and to dodge his men so successfully, he figured Growler had to have been hiking back and forth between checkpoints. If his theory was true, he wondered what would motivate someone to change his direction so often.

Growler just grumbled. "Where's everybody else?"

"What do you mean?" asked Gear Junkie. "Aren't Tracker and Streaming with you?"

"I don't know where they are. I haven't seen them since last night. They're probably still asleep."

Lana Lang had enough. "I told you so," she grumbled. She ordered one more coffee and announced she was leaving. "If you want to come with me, fine, and if the others are smart enough to remember the name of the farm, maybe they'll show up eventually. I don't care. Besides, I'm only staying there a couple of days. That should give the cops enough time to find the killer."

Growler managed to talk her into waiting long enough for him to get a coffee.

"You've got two minutes." While she was using the restroom and out of earshot, Growler ordered The Beanery's special Lumberjack Breakfast of eggs, toast, hash browns, and ham.

"Make that to go," he added gruffly. He awkwardly fished around in his jacket for cash, but his pocket was so crammed with stuff, when he finally yanked out a loose twenty-dollar bill, he didn't notice that a large bundle of money came out with it. When the wad fell to the floor, it fanned out to reveal a few hundred dollars in crisp tens and twenties. He was still oblivious to his loss as he walked back to the table.

"Hey, Donald Trump!" came Becky's wise-cracking voice from across the room. "You just dropped all this. Don't know about you, but we all work pretty hard for our money around here these days." She glared at Growler, who watched her pile it on her serving tray. "What? I have to pick it up and deliver it, too?" She stormed across the room and plopped the tray on his table.

If Growler wanted to attract attention, he couldn't have done a better job than he did with this spectacle in front of the restaurant full of customers. Looking embarrassed, he mumbled a faint thank you and pressed a bill into Becky's hand.

"Wow. A whole dollar! Gee, thanks! At least we know you're not that missing billionaire."

The people at the other tables burst into laughter, but Growler didn't understand the joke.

"I'll explain later," said Gear Junkie.

Growler doubled down and gave her another dollar. As he slung on his backpack, he heard the cashier's loud announcement, "Marion, your order is ready!"

He knocked over his chair, racing to the cashier. "Hey, don't shout my name!"

"Marion?" snickered Lana Lang. "Your name is Marion?"

As the cashier handed him his take out, the bell jingled again, and when a man and woman in uniform entered, Growler's face turned white. He dropped the Styrofoam takeout box on the counter and whispered to the cashier that he'd be back. Then, trying to appear nonchalant, he hurried toward the kitchen and slipped through the swinging doors. Before anyone noticed, he raced out the back of the restaurant.

The two officers made a quick survey of the room before taking their seats at a table in the window. "Becky, can we have some of your famous coffee, please?"

When Growler didn't return, Lana Lang called to the cashier, "Hey, where did Marion go?" Without looking up, the cashier pointed with her thumb in the direction of the kitchen, and Lana Lang stormed through the swinging doors. She returned seconds later without him and announced she was leaving. She grabbed her backpack and headed for the door, leaving Gear Junkie at the table.

"Hey, wait for me!" he yelled as he scooped up his things and ran to pay his bill. While he stood in line, he casually glanced around the room, and just as it became his turn, he saw the man who had participated so much in the conversation earlier turn to face him.

"Mr. Apple?"

Alain de la Pomme nodded and motioned that it was okay for Gear Junkie to get on his way without stopping to say hello.

"Okay, see you around," said Gear Junkie, and he hustled back over to join Lana Lang, who was already halfway out the door.

"Hey, guess what? I just ran into Mr. Apple."

"Yeah, who cares?"

"Well, then what about Growler?"

"What about him?"

The door slammed behind them.

Tinkle, slap, tinkle.

After a five-minute lull while the patrons of The Beanery continued acting like customers, Alain announced, "Great job everyone! That's a wrap for now. Stay in costume. We'll need you very soon."

Chapter 17

The slanted cat's eyes of the kitchen clock darted left and right, in sync with its sequined pendulum tail. Seven o'clock and Moonbeam was hungover. For her, the head pounding was a first and an inauspicious start to their day, though discovering the hostel provided breakfast helped with the transition. It was hardly the five a.m. departure they planned, but at least they wouldn't have to add to the delay by stopping to eat on the way.

Until they heard water running in the bathroom in the morning, the owners of the hostel often didn't realize they had guests, but Moonbeam had been there for several days, first with one man and now with a different one. They were starting to feel uncomfortable about having her around and planned to give her one more night before reporting her as a prostitute.

In the twenty years or so they'd owned the Shenandoah Hostel, hundreds of hikers had passed through their kitchen, but none looked like these two. They were stunned by the number of piercings on the young man's face, ears, and neck and knew they'd be giggling for years over others they speculated were in places they couldn't see. No wonder he called himself Hardware.

Their appearance was only the half of it. The girl with the multicolored hair sat at the table with her head in her hands. She complained of a terrible headache, yet she babbled incessantly. Now and then she would stop and look up. Then she would shake her head to say how the night before she had been a very bad girl and Hardware had been a very bad boy. The owners preferred hikers like Lana Lang. She arrived late, left early, and minded her own business while she was there. Sensing an endless waste of the morning, the owners made excuses and headed for their private apartment.

"Hey, wait!" Moonbeam called out. "Do you know if the trail is back open?"

"Back open? We didn't know it was closed."

Moonbeam and Hardware found the turn to the steps leading up to St. Peter's Catholic Church and the entrance to the Appalachian Trail after a short hike down High Street. At that early hour, they had to admire the church's stained-glass windows from the outside since the doors of St. Peter's wouldn't open until hours later. Instead of a tour of the inside, Moonbeam commemorated their stop with an outdoor selfie. The view of the Shenandoah River from the church was as breathtaking as she'd read in the guidebook, and they stopped to sit and enjoy the view a little longer, at least long enough for the aspirin to kick in. After thirty minutes or so her headache abated, and they decided it was time to take on the infamous sixty-four steps up to Jefferson Rock.

At about twenty steps up and to the right stood the charred brick ruins of St. John's Episcopal Church. With no roof, no door, and three and a half walls, unlike St. Paul's, this was a church that would always be open to visitors. They left the steps and walked the short distance to peek through one of the carefully restored brick rectangles that had once been a window. Then they followed the wall around to the entrance at the far end to the grassy, mud-packed ground that once served as the nave's floor.

Moonbeam remembered reading that the town used the church as a barracks and hospital during the Civil War. She closed her eyes and wandered the roofless remains in a sort of meditative trance, and through a series of single syllables, long pauses, and humming she revealed to Hardware that she was picking up its energy.

"Yes, yes. I feel the suffering." She walked a little farther before stopping suddenly. "Yes. I'm picking up the pain." She continued her walking meditation, making random turns. "Now I can feel...oops! Crap!" Her ethereal connection was interrupted when she stepped on a pile of feces. She begged Hardware to come to her rescue, and he helped scrape off the offending material with a sharp stick he fashioned with his virgin pocket knife. The odor was fierce, and she insisted on knowing what it was. She rummaged in her backpack to retrieve one of the guidebooks and quickly identified the little mound of defecation as *Odocoileus virginianus* — deer poop.

"Typically, the pellets will clump to form a solid scat," she read aloud from the book.

For Moonbeam, stepping in deer poop seemed a small price to pay for scoring such a deep connection to the fallen soldiers of the Civil War. She turned her back to Hardware, so he could replace the field guide in the designated pocket, and doing so, she noticed pieces of paper on the ground a little farther away.

"Litter," she sniffed. "We've got to pick it up."

Finding any amount of litter was rare on the Appalachian Trail, as she'd learned from the literature. *Leave No Trace!* was one of the mantras of the whole trail system. One could see it stamped on postcards and souvenirs everywhere. The slogan referred to a set of ethics that promoted stewardship of the outdoors. That included minimizing the impact of campfires and disposing of waste properly on the trail.

As she reached down to pick up the first piece, she caught the familiar pungent smell again. On the ground in front of them they recognized another pile of solid scat. This time it would not be necessary to consult a guidebook for identification. Wads of toilet paper scattered around left no room for doubt.

She knew just where to find her folding camp shovel, and Hardware reluctantly dug a few angled cuts into the ground and pried up the sod. They took turns kicking some human's number two and the toilet paper into the deep slits he'd made. Then they stomped the divot back down and refolded the shovel. She was glad they'd asked to be shown how to do it the day before in the Visitor Center.

"What kind of person would have left this mess? Certainly not a hiker." Seconds later, she had her answer. Crumpled into a ball next to a wall lay Growler's ugly scarf.

"What number step were we on, do you remember?" asked Moonbeam as they resumed their ascent.

Hardware was just starting to answer when the flapping wings of a large and menacing bird swooped close and startled him. He ducked and dove to the ground. Another bird circled low and threatening off to the left in the direction of Jefferson Rock. Hardware estimated its wingspan at close to two meters, and he swore the birds were hissing. Before he had time to dig out the field guide again, at least three more raptors flapped near them. Moonbeam heard more behind her, and she squealed in delight. *Cathartes aura* - turkey vultures - the book read. The descriptions and photos were unmistakable.

"See? I told you all those years of not eating meat would all come back to me with blessings." Moonbeam had read something about animals feeling safe in the presence of vegetarians. "I mean look at all the nature I've manifested already today!"

Hardware told Moonbeam he had to take a leak and he'd meet her up at the rock. When she reached the top of the steps, she saw the rustic Park Service sign with its lengthy but urgent inscription.

Welcome to Jefferson Rock, listed on the National Registry of Historic Places. Danger! Jefferson Rock is Unstable. Walking on, climbing, ascending, descending or traversing Jefferson Rock or its supporting base rock is prohibited [36 CFR 2.A (A) (5)]

Ignoring the warning, she walked closer for a better view. The gleaming flat slab of shale stretched majestically atop four little red sandstone pillars, which in turn rested upon the largest in a pile of boulders. But it was not the formation or the otherwise stunning view that would be etched in her memory forever. That honor went to the figure wedged into a shallow crevice on one side, being feasted upon by six or eight frenzied vultures. By now, its juicy eyes had been pecked out and its face was bloodied and unrecognizable. Still, no field guide would be necessary. Tattered blue jeans identified the mammal before her.

Homo sapiens sapiens.

Chapter 18

<T hat story you planted about the bears was vintage de la Pomme. Glad to see you're back in the game. Is the farm going to come in handy?

>An apple orchard was a nice touch. It makes my alias more fun. Speaking of disguises, I ditched the wig. Doesn't fit very well anymore.

<Ha ha. It never did.

>Do you have a description for me, yet?

<I've got something even better. And worse. Are you sitting down?

>Uh-oh.

<No way to sugar coat this, friend. We just connected some new dots. There is no surrogate. The one we're looking for down there really is Le Mauvais. Sorry. I just can't explain how he got through our net.

>He's been right in front of me this whole time?

PART III

Chapter 19

Gear Junkie hustled to keep up with Lana Lang. Not that she'd set such a fast pace. She was just too energetic for him so early in the day. A police car swerved to their road from the highway and screamed toward town. As soon as it passed, she quickened her pace. Finally, when she stopped momentarily at an intersection, he caught up close enough to ask her. "Shouldn't we wait for Growler?"

"You can," she said in her typical brusque style. "But I'm getting out of this place."

Gear Junkie pressed her. "Come on, aren't you the least bit curious why he left in such a hurry?"

"Are you dense? The cops came. He split. Do the math."

"You seem like you're in a hurry, too. What's your excuse?"

She turned around and was about to answer, when she winced. Her hand went quickly to the back of her head. "Some jerk threw a rock or something at me."

"Not a rock, a beer can." Gear Junkie spotted the hunk of crumpled aluminum on the ground behind her.

"Psst, Lana Lang. Over here!" They spun around to catch Growler waving his arms from his hiding place behind a dumpster, asking them if the coast was clear. She gave him the finger and took off up the road again.

Gear Junkie yelled to him, "I can see the highway from here. If you hurry, we can get there with no trouble."

Growler tiptoed out from behind the dumpster, and after double checking to see if he was alone, he ran to catch up.

When they reached the highway, it was Growler's idea to use Lana Lang as bait for a ride, and he gave her an awkward demonstration on how to stick her thumb out and look sexy.

"I know how to hitchhike, you moron."

Growler sniffed at the rebuke, but let it go. He was in a hurry, and he dashed into the weeds on the side the road with Gear Junkie to hide from view. While they were squatting, Growler's stomach growled again, and he asked Gear Junkie if he had brought his takeout.

"No, but what the hell, Growler? Why didn't you bring it yourself? What's the matter with you?"

Growler didn't have to answer, because Lana Lang and her thumb had attracted a ride. A beat-up maroon pickup with a *South of the Border* sticker plastered on the bumper pulled over and slowed to a stop.

"Where to, little lady?" shouted the driver through the half-open passenger window.

"You heard of a place called Ridgefield Farm?" Just then, several squad cars whizzed past, and the screaming of their sirens made it impossible to hear her. High intensity flashing lights from their roof racks added another layer of chaos and distraction. The truck driver cupped a hand around his ear and asked her to repeat.

"I'm going to Ridgefield Farm," she shouted over the noise. "Do you know where it is?"

Another speeding police car and then another joined in the wailing and the flashing. They came from different directions, but all headed to Harpers Ferry. The strobes were blinding, and the noise was deafening. Finally, the driver gave up and reached across the cab and opened the passenger door.

Growler and Gear Junkie bolted from their hiding spot and all three tossed their things into the truck bed. Lana Lang pushed and shoved the others out of the way to claim the front seat, leaving Gear Junkie to squeeze into the back of the cab with Growler. Without checking if he was completely inside, she slammed the passenger door shut, nearly crushing Gear Junkie's foot. Instantly, the cab interior was quiet.

"Hey, guys. A hitchhiker pretending to hide from the driver is the oldest trick in the book. I knew she wasn't traveling alone," said the driver. He passed Ridgefield Farm every day and said he hoped it would be all right to drop them off at the entrance. His complexion was rough and littered with scars. A well-worn cowboy hat sat atop a thick mop of blond hair. He told them they were lucky he picked them up, since starting now the cops weren't letting anyone in or out of Harpers Ferry for a while. Then he laughed. "The name's Frank. So, which one of you is the missing billionaire?"

"None of us. He's dead," said Lana Lang.

"Oh, so he is the guy they found. No wonder there are so many cop cars."

"My friend here is wrong," said Gear Junkie. "Nobody said the victim was the billionaire."

"Well, what do we know about the dead person?"

Gear Junkie gave him a quick description. "Tall guy, early thirties."

Frank understood someone killed the guy by snapped the man's neck. "That's pretty gruesome. Got any other details?"

Gear Junkie added a little more about the victim's tent and confirmed that the police called it a homicide. "We got the story last night, straight from a police scanner."

"Huh? What do you mean last night?"

"The waitress told us during dinner at the White Horse."

"Sorry guys, that's impossible. They found the dead guy this morning, so I'd say you heard that wrong."

Lana Lang piped in. "It has to be the same person. How many murders could there be on the Appalachian Trail in forty-eight hours? But I still don't understand why they would close off Harpers Ferry, considering they found the body on the trail."

"The Shady Pines shelter?" Frank sounded incredulous. "No, no. Wrong again, I'm afraid. Or we're talking about two different people. The dead body I'm talking about was right here in town, up at Jefferson Rock. Two hikers found him."

"What?!" Gear Junkie poked his ashen face into the front seat.

Frank said he hoped he was mistaken, and he called his wife to straighten it out. When a woman somewhere answered on speakerphone, he got to the point. "Honey, didn't you tell me they found the body in Harpers Ferry this morning? I'm with some hikers who are telling me a different story. They said the murder happened at Shady Pines campground. Which one is it?"

"My stars, Frank. Both. It's all over the news. They found one at the shelter last night. And this morning, they found another one at Jefferson Rock. I swear I told you at breakfast."

Gear Junkie panicked. "My god. Another murder. Hey Frank, ask her if she has a description of the person they found this morning. I'm worried it could be a friend of ours."

"Am I on your speaker? Listen to me, Frank, a big thunderstorm is on the way, so I need you stop at the store and get some milk and toilet paper, okay? And promise me you won't pick up any more hitchhikers on the way. There's a madman loose around here."

Frank took the call off speaker and mumbled that the hikers were about to get out. As soon as everyone grabbed their gear, he floored it and sped off in a spray of gravel, leaving the passenger door still open and flapping. In seconds, his truck was over a hill and out of sight.

"Man, I was hoping he would take us back to town. He didn't even wait for us to thank him for the ride," said Gear Junkie, staring at the empty road. When he turned around, he discovered he'd been talking to himself. Lana Lang and Growler were already heading down the farm's long driveway. When he caught up, Growler asked who they were supposed to see about the jobs.

"What do you mean, the jobs? You aren't serious about staying here after what the truck driver told us? We've got to go back. Somebody got killed at Jefferson Rock last night, and it might be one of our friends."

Lana Lang dismissed him. "Look, they weren't my friends. I just met them. Anyway, why would anyone want to kill idiot nobodies like Tracker or Streaming?"

"I'm not going all the way back," said Growler. "They were both alive when I left. If they're dead, there's nothing we can do."

Gear Junkie was in a hurry to return to town, but as he walked toward the road, he made one last attempt at cheerleading. "So, who's coming with me, huh?"

Gear Junkie had become so invested in trying to convince the others, he hadn't noticed he was standing in the road. *Honk! Honk!* The driver of the speeding car slammed on the horn and swerved to avoid hitting him. Startled by the blare, he lurched to one side and fell into a drainage ditch. The fall didn't hurt him, but the deep pool of standing water soaked his pants.

It was starting to mist. And according to Frank's wife, it would turn to a storm very soon.

Chapter 20

After initial tests proved inconclusive, the lab team decided to pack it in for the day. They knew the device could track something, but they weren't clear just what. Dr. Lambiel, the lead scientist, had just finished reassembling the arcane device for the night, when his lab assistant popped in on her way out.

"I can tell you're frustrated, and I thought I'd pass on some advice my grandfather gave me when he couldn't find a solution. I don't know if I told you, but he was a famous scientist, too. Anyway, he called it his 'out of sight, out of mind' strategy. He'd put the problem aside and forget about it for a while," she explained as she closed the door. She immediately stuck her head back in. "Oh, and don't forget your meeting in South Lab starts in five minutes."

Dr. Lambiel thanked her for the reminder, but not for the advice. Tired old sayings like the one from her grandfather rubbed him the wrong way. As he popped the casing back on the device, he wished her a good evening instead. He checked his watch and determined he could still be on time. South Lab was an unsecured building, and he wouldn't need to waste time presenting credentials at multiple security checks like he did in his part of the complex.

He'd already locked the vault for the evening, and since he was running late, he didn't want to take the time to reopen it. Instead, he dropped the gadget into his coat pocket for safe-keeping and hustled across the campus.

The meeting was in progress when the last pair of automatic doors slid apart, and he apologized profusely as he strode across the room to take his seat at the round table with the others. He'd been so rushed he didn't notice something buzzing from inside his lab jacket. They assumed he'd forgotten to silence his mobile phone, and they pointed to his pocket. He retrieved the device he'd forgotten he was carrying. Squawking sounds and pulsing beeps poured from the otherwise silent earbuds. When he put them in his ears, the real analysis began.

Like a child being told he is getting warmer or colder, Dr. Lambiel wandered around the lab following the hanging intensity of sound.

"Voilà!" he announced, stopping at a lab workstation. The setup looked like an electronics lab anywhere. Abandoned components piled high, with wires connecting things to each other with alligator clips.

"Can someone please tell me whose bench this is, and what they are working on?" he asked the room.

The rest of them crowded around, but they couldn't offer much help. The scientist who had occupied it quit after only working three months. While he impressed the others with his brilliance, he had problems getting a security clearance, and his bench was currently unoccupied.

"Well, something here is causing this thing to talk to me," he said, thrilled at the breakthrough.

Lambiel postponed the rest of the agenda to give priority to his gadget. He ordered everything on the bench examined, and one by one, each item from the bench was removed from the room. When the device continued to emit noises at the same decibel level even after the last piece of equipment had been taken out of range, he was confused.

All that remained was a small office pencil holder containing the usual random collection of ballpoint pens and the odd paperclip. Again, they systematically removed the items, and exasperated at the continued beeping, he finally overturned the pencil holder and dumped the remaining contents on the countertop.

A few more paper clips bounced and spread out revealing the culprit — a small unused GeoFibre clothing label, embroidered with the letters, WFCDLP. When they removed it from the room, the gadget became quiet. There was no longer any doubt as to the purpose of the device. Someone designed it to find Will.

By the end of the evening, Dr. Lambiel had prepared the device for shipping, with instructions and a new battery charger. He also inserted a note explaining the device was assembled at their own GeoFibre lab in Montreux. Within hours, it was bound for Harpers Ferry and the hands of Alain de la Pomme, the man who discovered it.

WORKERS THIS WAY. The hand-painted wooden sign at the end of the farm's driveway pointed toward the back of a barn, where a tall scarecrow with a smiling face gave further directions: "Hikers wait here."

"Oh, great," groused Lana Lang, eyeing the heavy wooden picnic table. "Another *hiker table.*"

They didn't have to wait long before an ancient and rusty one-eyed Land Rover rumbled down from the other side of the barn. Squeaky brakes accompanied an impressive backfire and a cloud of black smoke when it slammed to a stop in front of their table. The dented driver's side door let out a screech when a young Hispanic with straight, shiny black shoulder-length hair bounded out.

Growler got to his feet and assumed his tough guy attitude. "We're here for a job," he demanded gruffly, shoving a determined face inches away from the Hispanic. "Who do we see?"

The response blasted back in ninety seconds of rapid-fire Spanish, complete with wild, animated hand gestures. Caught by surprise and completely disarmed, Growler sat back down. After a moment he uttered a weak protest. "Me no habla Spanish."

Unfazed, the young Hispanic pointed to their gear and motioned to follow him. When they reached a clearing, he pointed to the gathering storm clouds and rattled off another two or three minutes of explanation, also in Spanish.

Confused, Growler looked to Lana Lang for empathy. "Can you believe this guy? How are we supposed to know what to do now?"

"You dope. He told us to pitch our tents in the clearing over near the outhouse."

"Wait, you speak Spanish? Why didn't you say so?"

"God, you are such a loser!" she snapped.

The Hispanic then first pointed to Growler's backpack and then to a spot about twenty feet away. "Tent," he said to Growler slowly. "You put."

The farm's shabby condition wasn't what Growler expected. The designated campsite occupied one end of a large and decrepit garden about thirty yards by a hundred. Weeds had overtaken the raised beds, and morning glories strangled the patchwork deer fencing that surrounding the space on three sides. Next to an old-fashioned hand pump, what looked to be a former chicken coop now served as the communal outhouse and listed precariously to one side.

"What's the password for the Wi-Fi?" asked Lana Lang in Spanish.

The Hispanic explained that there wasn't a signal where they stood, but she might have better luck closer to the house. But doling out the password came from the boss, and she'd have to ask him when he returned. He excused himself and walked back to the car.

"Did you ask him about the Wi-Fi?"

"Of course, but the signal doesn't reach here. He said he didn't know the password, but I'm not sure I believe him. Anyway, it'll only take me two minutes to hack. It will be something dumb like *farm*. Even you should be able to figure it out."

"Hey, well at least we're off the trail and away from all the cops."

She sniffed. "Look, I'm not a fan of the police either, but at least I'm not running from them."

Growler bombarded her with questions. He was eager to know if the Mexican mentioned anything about how much they paid.

"They're paying us a hundred dollars a day. His name is Alvaro, and he's from Chile, not Mexico," she corrected. "And get this straight. From now on, I'm not your translator."

"Whatever." He was thrilled. A hundred a day was a lot of money, but he hoped that the high pay didn't mean the work would be hard.

The mist turned to a sprinkle as Lana Lang carried her gear to a spot in the far corner of the clearing. Her tent was up in minutes, and she positioned it for maximum privacy, with the zippered door flap facing away from the rest of the campsite. Growler followed with his gear and plopped it down next to her.

"Find your own spot!" she shooed him away through the flap. "I don't want you anywhere near me."

Unleashing a string of expletives, he dragged his gear to a

spot on the other side of the outhouse. He was tired of her attitude, but it wasn't Lana Lang he was cursing. It was having to set up his tent, always his least favorite thing to do. And now he had to put it up in the rain.

He fumbled with it, but his non-proficiency had little to do with the rain. The tent had met the same fate as every other piece of gear he bought. He barely took the time to pull things out of their boxes before cramming them in his crappy little backpack. In his haste, he had thrown away the instructions to everything along with the packaging.

The metal stakes were like his tent, flimsy and cheap, and he snapped one in half on the first night, when he used a rock for a hammer. The ones that didn't break, bent. The second night when he carelessly shoved things back into his pack too fast and too hard, he broke one of the tent poles, and ever since the tent listed to one side and sagged in the middle. Even the zipper was substandard. After zipping it open and closed only twice, the front flap stuck in the open position. But those were inconveniences he could live without fixing. A permanent drawback was its size, two feet too short for a man of his height. He probably should have taken the salesman's advice.

Buying his camping gear came down to twenty tense minutes in a big box store not far away in northeastern Pennsylvania. A young sales associate said Growler was lucky, because he could give him some serious product advice, being a hiker, too. But Growler was impatient and didn't have time to listen to anyone's expertise.

"So, what do you need?" asked the salesman.

"Everything."

The teenager laughed. "I'm sure that's not true. Let's start with what you have."

"I don't have a thing."

They would start with the tent, and he motioned for Growler to follow him to another aisle, where he found more styles and sizes than he cared to know about. The associate tried to get him to talk about the climate and terrain Growler would encounter, but he ignored him. He grabbed the first one he saw with a discount tag and threw it into his shopping cart. It was on sale for $39.95.

"I want the cheapest one" became his emphatic mantra and the standard rebuttal to almost every item the salesman would suggest.

The young man wanted to show Growler some other essential items. "You'll need a tarp, a cook set, and a canteen. They're over in aisle twenty-eight." When Growler asked him what a cook set was, the young man's response belied his astonishment. "You know, pots and pans."

"Pots and pans? Are you kidding? I'm not going to be cooking. What are you on? Commission?"

The associate looked confused, but he sensed his customer getting testy, and he didn't want to lose the sale. Growler was impatient and resented having to waste time going back and forth between aisles. He had already spent ten minutes shopping, and since he still needed to buy clothes, he told the kid to pick out the rest of the stuff by himself.

"But what time of the year are you going?" the kid asked him as he left for the clothing department. "Because it really matters, if..."

"Today." Growler was adamant. "Now. I'm leaving as soon as we're done!"

Two store security guards talking in the next aisle caused him to make a long detour. When he got back to the camping department with a couple extra T-shirts, socks, and a cheap hooded sweatshirt, he found the young salesman had done his job. His cart was full. Still, he snapped at the kid. "How am I supposed to carry all this?"

The young man smiled and held out the large backpack he'd selected, which Growler rejected after a glance at the price tag.

Knocking it to the floor, his hands went straight to the cheapest one, and without a word of thanks to the helpful clerk, he wheeled his cart toward the checkout.

On the way, he tossed half the items onto random shelves and into bins containing other merchandise. What was the kid thinking? A hatchet? He wouldn't be chopping wood. It landed in a bin of ladies lingerie. He kept the headlamp because it would be valuable for hiking at night. He acknowledged it was the only valuable piece of advice the boy gave him. At checkout, he threw two dozen candy bars and ten bags of chips onto the conveyor belt. A quick look at the running total on the register made him rethink his purchases, and at the last minute, he removed the toilet paper and an extra pack of batteries.

"Sign here, please," said the cashier. Growler was relieved when the charge went through. He hoped the amount was under the threshold that would send an alert to the credit card's owner, and deciding not to press his luck further, he dropped the card in a trashcan on his way out.

Long ago he'd learned the skills to avoid being captured on store security cameras, and he hustled head down to the far end of the parking lot. As soon as he got in the dented Mercedes, that week's ride, he started to stuff his purchases in the cheap pack. He still had too much stuff, and fitting everything in was frustrating, so he dumped a few things out the car window. Twenty miles later, he was beyond the city limits and headed southwest as far as the gas tank would carry him.

The car's navigation system led him to an entrance to the Appalachian Trail from the highway and his path to temporary obscurity. He locked the car and tossed the keys into the woods.

Ten minutes in and he knew he'd made a mistake. Disappearing on the trail was going to be more work than he imagined. A half mile from where he entered, the path ascended a steep ridge and walking became strenuous. After two miles, he was dying of thirst. His backpack weighed a ton, even after dumping so many things in the parking lot. Somehow, he needed to figure out how to endure it for a few weeks. He hoped by then he would be out of the woods, both figuratively and literally.

Distance was never his objective. His goal was only to keep moving and stay out of sight. After two-and-a-half weeks on the trail, he'd covered many miles but hadn't gone far. He hadn't thought to pick up a map, and since he'd tossed the compass the salesman said he'd need into a bin of toilet brushes in Aisle 6, he ended up hiking back and forth over the same stretch of trail without realizing it. He started out heading south, but after the second night, he forgot which direction he was hiking and ended up going back in the direction he came.

To avoid being seen, he hiked at night and slept by day - in shelters if he was lucky. That way he wouldn't have to mess with his tent. When he found a good one, he stayed a couple nights. What constituted being a good shelter had nothing to do with its condition or its facilities or its view, but one that was unoccupied.

Now, as he was forcing in the final tent stake, he spotted Lana Lang exiting the outhouse. He had to hand it to her; she was brave. No way would he ever set foot in that place, especially now since she used it. Anyway, he'd gotten used to pooping in the woods.

THOUGH THE RAIN was light but steady, Lana Lang determined to connect to the farm's Wi-Fi signal and didn't mind. She protected her phone inside her rain slicker and kept it in a zipped bag so she could monitor the signal strength icon through the clear plastic. Like a rat wandering an invisible maze, she zig-zagged the quarter mile to the house, tracing the changes in strength. Finally, she stopped under the thick umbrella of a large old maple tree close to the barn. Leaning against its smooth trunk, her fingers flew over the keypad. "Ha!" she muttered after only a few minutes. "*Farm123*. I knew it!"

Then she slipped into the barn, just in time, too, because the rain quickly turned torrential. Once inside she entered the door Alvaro described which led to the interior accommodations. On either side of the narrow hallway were small motel like bedrooms, each complete with a television. None was occupied, so she selected the room with the strongest Wi-Fi signal. The outlet next to the bed was a plus, too. Now she could keep her phone charged while she relaxed and caught up on messages she missed since logging in at the Hiker Lounge. She swiped through her usual websites and suddenly froze. A familiar face looked back.

Chapter 21

Suzen called Alain with an update. Her engineers concluded someone sabotaged the system by introducing a virus with a simple thumb drive to the controlling server, which GeoFibre housed in an underutilized facility in western Maryland, twenty miles from Harpers Ferry. The building's location was not technically a secret, but it was unmarked, and whoever broke in could only have learned how to find it from someone inside the company. The tip about a newly installed outdoor security camera system likely came from the same insider.

But the saboteur wasn't aware of an important update. A defect in the camera lens caused a major delay, and the system he thought he'd disabled hadn't been activated. The previous camera captured everything, and since the engineers could tell exactly when the perpetrator injected the virus, Suzen would easily and quickly find a usable closeup of the perpetrator using the video's timecode.

She was upbeat. "So, do you think the same guy could have done everything?"

"Now that we know it's Le Mauvais, I'm sure he's working alone. Our server is so close to the Shady Pines campsite, he could have popped in the thumb drive and made it up there on the same day in plenty of time to commit his murder."

"I can't believe we had a spy inside GeoFibre. Maybe we still do. How could we not know?"

"We'll soon find out. I've got the security team combing through the camera footage now. I should have a blowup for us any minute."

"I am eager to see how the image matches up with our suspects. As an agent of Interpol, I have the authority I need to bring the perpetrator into custody. Our footage will give me all the evidence we need. Connecting him to the murder will require more proof. Lana Lang and Growler are at the farm already, and we're going to bring the rest of them out there later today. We can't keep them at the farm forever, so I hope to shake somebody loose at tonight's picnic."

"I realize I've asked you before, but are you sure you have all the suspects? Seems like there would have been more people on the trail."

"We were lucky it was off season. No, this is everyone. There were a couple of families out for a day in the mountains, but we cleared them quickly."

Suzen didn't sound convinced. "What about all the hikers who were staying in the hostel? I thought the place was full. Couldn't one of them be our assassin or the accomplice?"

"Sure, if they were real hikers." He laughed. "It didn't take many extras to make one small hostel seem full."

What he needed was the data she couldn't give him yet. He knew where Will's gear ended up but knowing exactly where and when it traveled would help him reconstruct the chain of events and eliminate some of the hikers from suspicion. The inability to access it was frustrating, but the virus had been unchecked for several days, and the damage was considerable. Their most senior team of experts was working around the clock, in some cases rebuilding much of the code from scratch.

"I seeded the Patrick Myers Memorial Fund in memory of Streaming with a half million dollars," said Suzen. "I made the contribution anonymous, as you requested and directed one hundred percent of the proceeds to the family."

Alain was devasted when he heard someone murdered the young man. Streaming was a good kid, and Alain grieved for his family. He and Will vowed to do as much as they could to help them with their pain. But before sending his body home, Alain ordered it whisked to a nearby private underground installation on six hundred acres along the Potomac River. A quick and quiet autopsy revealed the unsurprising cause of death: cervical fracture.

While it shocked him to learn that Le Mauvais had killed again so soon and so brazenly, the desperate action convinced Alain it was a signal the killer felt trapped. The young man must have witnessed something on the trail that Le Mauvais did not want revealed to the police, and fortunately, Streaming got to them early.

More than anything, Alain was grief-stricken that Streaming had escaped his protection. The kid didn't have as much as a moving violation to his name, and Alain never considered him a suspect or a worry, and certainly not at-risk. He was sorry he let Will talk him into remaining at arm's length after dinner, but he knew Streaming's death wasn't his nephew's fault either. Streaming was in the right place at the wrong time, and Alain now worried that his nephew wasn't out of the woods yet.

Chapter 22

Will started looking for Gear Junkie almost as soon as he dropped him off. He could tell Gear Junkie worried about the well-being of Tracker and Streaming, and he had a hunch his friend would want to get back to Harpers Ferry quickly. With so few hikers on the trail, Gear Junkie was right to assume the body was one of his friends, especially since neither had turned up at breakfast.

By the time Will caught up with him, it was nearly forty-five minutes later, and Gear Junkie was almost to the farm entrance. Will figured he'd either changed his mind about leaving or he had lost his way and was backtracking. Between the racket of the sirens and the intense conversation "Frank" was having with the hikers, it was understandable that Gear Junkie hadn't paid attention to the turns.

Gear Junkie was moving fast, probably because of the serious storm Frank said was sure to roll in soon. He was already soaking, though, which Will knew couldn't have been from the light drizzle. When Gear Junkie saw him, he stuck his thumb out, and Will rumbled to a stop.

"Quick, hop in," Will said. "I'll give you a ride, but you have to promise not to tell my wife. She'd kill me if she found out I was still picking up hitchhikers."

"I didn't expect to see you again, Frank," said Gear Junkie. "Sorry about the wet clothes. I fell into a puddle."

"No worries. I was on the road, because I forgot to buy toilet paper. And since a maniac running around is scaring my wife, she added ammunition to my list."

COMPARED to the chaotic scene at the turnoff, by noon there was only one cop car in sight, and the town of Harpers Ferry was doornail dead. Since his team convinced the few hikers they rounded up they couldn't leave town, Alain no longer needed to put on quite the show at the highway. One squad car sufficed to keep up the pretense of a blockade. Today he wanted to learn what he could from the ones still in town, before he connived them into going to the farm later. With more information, and all of them in the same place, he hoped he could maneuver the assassin into revealing himself.

In the meantime, he learned Gear Junkie was safely in the truck and just entering town. The Beanery would be the perfect stage for the intervention. Besides, another café au lait was just what Alain needed to clear his head. He was glad he thought to pop for an elaborate coffee machine for the restaurant's kitchen. As often as he would frequent the joint, he'd need a proper cup, something otherwise impossible to come by in the little town.

Alain was on his phone when Gear Junkie appeared, and Alain gestured for him to have a seat. He asked Gear Junkie to order him a coffee and whatever else he wanted for himself, while he finished the call.

"By the way, you look terrible. Oh, and you stink. Give me a minute, will you? I'll be right back." He chuckled as he left.

Compared to the drunken wino act he put on the night before, he must have appeared very sophisticated to the young man.

Alain watched Gear Junkie from afar, hoping to catch his reaction to the absence of the flyer that littered the restaurant in the morning. Gear Junkie ran his fingers through his mussed hair and snuck away to the restroom. When he came back, his hair was more orderly, and he'd wiped the mud from his legs. He tried to get Becky's attention, but she dashed past with orders for everyone else.

"Excuse me, coffee?" Gear Junkie asked, raising his voice.

"I see you," she said, banging through the swinging doors. She disappeared into the kitchen.

Gear Junkie walked over to the cashier, explained he'd been waiting for quite a while, and asked if it was okay to serve himself.

"Your waitstaff will take your order," she clarified, without looking up from her iPhone. He gave a little sigh and walked back to his booth empty handed.

This torture had gone on long enough, and Alain slid in to join his young friend. "What made you change tables?"

Gear Junkie told him the story about falling into the ditch and landing on sharp rocks. "My butt took quite a beating this morning, and these booths looked more comfortable."

"It must feel luxurious." Alain couldn't suppress another laugh. "Hey, weren't you going to get me a coffee?"

"Sorry, Mr. Apple, I've been trying. It's like the waitress is ignoring me on purpose."

"Allow me." He turned his head ever so slightly toward Becky and gave her a nearly imperceptible nod. As if by some magnetic force, her eyes suddenly turned toward his, and though they spoke no words, less than a minute later she returned with menus and two coffees. Gear Junkie wanted to know how Mr. Apple did it.

"One day maybe I'll share my secret. In the meantime, I

thought you were off to work on a farm today. What changed your mind?"

Gear Junkie took a breath. "It's a long story, but before I forget, I want to thank you for buying dinner last night. You surprised us all. Sorry I couldn't speak with you this morning. It was a little awkward with the others."

"Oh, I completely understand. I noticed Lana Lang was in a rush, but points for remembering to say thank you."

"So today I'm treating you."

"That's very nice. Thank you. Now what about your long story?"

"It's about the new body they found this morning."

"Yes, the tragic news about Jefferson Rock is the talk of the town. And so soon after that other grisly murder at the shelter."

Gear Junkie told Alain about the night before and how his friends hadn't turned up that morning. Revealing he was the last one to see them alive was naïve but refreshingly honest. Alain pushed him farther. "Oh, so you don't know who the body is yet? Well, maybe I can find out. Was there something else?"

"Actually, yes. Remember those flyers that were everywhere this morning? I noticed they're gone now. Do you think it means somebody identified the body? Then there's this whole other thing about William de la Pomme being missing."

"Ah, yes, de la Pomme, the other talk of the town. You seem to know a lot about him. Something about studying him in college?"

"I did a paper on him for a business course. In fact, my dream has been to work at a company like his one day." He leaned to whisper. "This might sound callous, Mr. Apple, because I realize those dead bodies are somebody's friends and relatives, but I hope they turn out to be someone else. I'd really like to see him walk in here right now. The world could use a few more de la Pommes."

"I'd very much like to see him walk in now, myself," said

Alain. He motioned for a refill and changed the subject. "Did I overhear you have an MBA?"

His finances hadn't permitted Gear Junkie to finish, but he was only short a semester. He had gotten discouraged and was using his time on the trail to sort out his next steps.

"Economics isn't always fair," said Alain. "But let's get back to that long tale of yours. It sounds like I left the restaurant too early and missed a lot."

Gear Junkie told him the whole story, beginning with how surprised everyone was to learn he'd picked up their tabs. He described how Moonbeam and Hardware had gotten very drunk and had gone directly to the hostel. And how everyone else went up to Jefferson Rock.

"What about the girl, Lana Lang? Did she join you?"

"No. She didn't want anything to do with us. I assumed she stayed at the hostel with the others."

"I hate to interrupt, but you and Streaming were friends, am I right? I remember you came into the restaurant together."

Gear Junkie shrugged. "Not really. We were both alone but happened to be hiking a part of the trail at the same time. That's how we ended up here together. Even so, I never got to know him. He always wore his earbuds, so there was never much conversation." Then he related the story of catching Tracker at the last minute before going off the ledge.

"Wow, you're quite the hero."

"That's what he said. He even promised to pay me back for it one day."

"What on earth could Tracker do for you? He doesn't appear to be someone with many resources. If he were sitting here, I'd advise him to spend money on an orthodontist first, wouldn't you agree?"

"He was probably drunk when he said it, and I don't expect to hear from him again. But gee, like he said, I saved his life. I'd hate it if he ended up dead up there after all that."

"Let's be positive and assume Tracker is not the one they found. Next time you see him, why don't you ask him to pay the rest of your business school tuition?"

Gear Junkie got a kick out of the gag, but he changed the subject back to William de la Pomme. "Can I run something past you? So, let's say he's not dead. If the rangers directed all of us hikers to Harpers Ferry, shouldn't he be here with the rest of us?"

"Yes, I suppose you are right. I never thought of that."

Becky arrived with the check and before she could spin around to leave, Gear Junkie asked her to stay. "Just out of curiosity, do you remember me? Because I have a question."

"Sure, hon. Of course, I remember. You were here this morning with that unpleasant woman and the big shot with all the money, who didn't tip worth a darn."

He gulped. "Wow, was that the impression I gave?"

"You are judged by the company you keep," Alain cautioned, citing the famous fable of Aesop. "But fear not. Reputations can be fixed."

"Anyway, hon, was that your question? Because I'm busy."

"No. I noticed somebody took down all the posters about the dead body in the shelter. Does that mean they found out who the guy was?"

"Sure does." She turned to go.

"Wait! Was it William de la Pomme?"

"The missing billionaire?" She moved to clear a nearby table. "Heavens, no. Turned out to be a local guy."

"Are you sure?"

"Positive."

"So, where do you suppose he is?"

"Who?"

"De la Pomme, the billionaire."

"How would I know? But they've got this whole town sealed off, so he's got to be around here somewhere. I hope he comes by. After your cheapskate friend, I could use a big tipper."

If Gear Junkie wasn't the killer, he was doing a good job of appearing like him with his probing questions about Will. Alain smiled at Becky and slipped her a twenty.

It was raining hard when they left The Beanery. Gear Junkie mentioned wanting to sleep in an actual bed for once, and he asked Mr. Apple for a lift to the hostel so he could reserve one. A *NO VACANCY* sign greeted them. The owners said they hadn't been this busy in years.

"Apparently, some bears scared all the hikers off the trail, and the authorities are putting everyone up here. It's always feast or famine."

They would have had a bed, but the couple who checked out that morning came back after discovering the dead body. They were understandably in shock, and the sympathetic owners gave them their room back. As if to put the request to rest, she laid the reservation list on the counter and secured it with a Jefferson Rock paperweight.

"I'm terribly sorry."

"What about the bunk we saved for the guy who never showed up?" asked her husband from across the room. "He still hasn't called, so I say we rent it to this guy."

Gear Junkie was ecstatic. "Thank you, person who never showed up. Because of you, this place will be my home sweet home for a while."

"Things will be a lot sweeter for everyone after you take a shower and do some laundry," joked Alain. He excused himself to take care of what he called pressing things. "I'll probably see you a little later. It's a nicety of a small town. People run into each other all the time."

Gear Junkie dropped his clothes in the washing machine on the way to the shower. The owners learned long ago it was better to offer free laundry service than put up with a building full of stinky hikers. As he reached for the handle, the shower door flung open, pushing him backward.

"Sorry," said the guy who emerged from the steam's opaqueness. "Wait a minute, Gear Junkie?"

"Tracker? You're alive! Man, am I glad to see you."

Chapter 23

"What are you talking about?" Will asked, hiding a smile. "Of course I'm alive. You saved my life, remember?"

"Well, yeah, but since you never showed up this morning, I thought you might be dead."

"Dead? Why?" Will pretended he no idea what Gear Junkie was talking about and suggested they had serious catching up to do. "But let's sit on the porch where it's more comfortable, and we can celebrate that I'm not dead."

Gear Junkie pointed to Will's head. "You don't really wear your hat in the shower, do you?"

"Not when the water's running, silly, but hey, it's my trademark," he joked. In reality, he wore it more as a precaution. Though the hat with the ponytail wig his uncle gave him was top of the line, he was still paranoid about being recognized. "And believe me, I wouldn't want you to see what I look like without it." As he stepped to the side to let Gear Junkie enter, he pinched his nose. "Phew! Where have you been? You stink."

On the way to his room, Will picked up a familiar voice. In the room next to his own, Hardware was sitting on a bed and making a rushed phone call. He spoke in German, no doubt so that nosy listeners wouldn't understand him, but Will did. "I'll meet you in Medellin as soon as I can. The Cipher project, right? I can't stay here another second. This woman is driving me crazy."

Gear Junkie was only wearing a towel when he got back to the dorm room, and he explained it would be awhile before he could join Will on the porch because he was washing all his clothes -- orders from Mr. Apple.

"Mr. Apple? You saw him again?" He tossed Gear Junkie a pair of his sweatpants and a t-shirt. "Here, you can put these on for now. Let's go."

The rain pummeled the roof of the wraparound porch. No one else was around, and he commandeered a whole seating area. "So, tell me about dear old Mr. Wino."

"Before we talk about him, first I want to find out if Streaming is alive or not."

"What do you mean? Why wouldn't he be?"

Gear Junkie filled him in with what little he knew about the second body, and how he had worried it was one of them. "Since Growler was at breakfast, and now you're alive, it only leaves Streaming unaccounted for. But I'm hoping it was someone completely different they found."

"Gosh, that's horrible! But now I get why you were worried."

"Where were you, by the way? We were expecting you at The Beanery. I mean, going to the farm was your idea, after all."

In reality, Will had spent a few hours in a chair, laying on the special effects makeup that would compose his Frank disguise. Quickly, he thought of an excuse. "I'm sorry, I overslept, and by the time I realized I'd missed the meetup, I decided I might as well go back to sleep. I've only been awake an hour, so this is all news to me."

"I figured you were hungover."

"Nah, I was drinking soda water all night. I'm kind of a light-weight in the alcohol department. In fact, I didn't even finish my one beer before I switched. I pretended to get a buzz along with everyone else because I didn't want to spoil the vibe."

"And here I thought I was the only sober one."

Will smiled. "Acting runs in my family."

"I guess so. You sure had me fooled, but I believe you now. In fact, you and Mr. Apple are the only people I trust around here."

It was time to apply some pressure. "I wish I could say the same about you."

Gear Junkie's face fell. "Huh? What do you mean?"

"Well, didn't you take my money? When I woke up, I noticed someone unzipped my backpack and took my cash. By then, Growler had left and Streaming was still asleep, so who else could it have been?" Of the two, Will thought Growler would take the bait, and he was surprised Gear Junkie was the culprit.

"Are you crazy? Of course I didn't take it."

Will laughed. "I mean, I remember saying you could have it, but I thought you understood I had to go over a cliff or something first."

"Maybe Growler came back up. Search my stuff, if you don't believe me."

"Okay, okay. I believe you. But somebody took it."

A maroon pickup truck pulled up in front of the hostel. The passenger door opened, and an umbrella popped open. Beneath it stood Alain de la Pomme as Mr. Apple, who dropped by under the pretext of connecting Gear Junkie to the Dean of the Business School at the local university. "His contact information is on this pamphlet, and he's expecting you to call."

Will tried to get his uncle up to speed. "Gear Junkie was just telling me the horrible news about somebody killed at Jefferson Rock last night, and we were hoping it wasn't Streaming." He filled them both in on what happened after Gear Junkie left. He'd only been asleep a short time when he heard someone dashing down the steps toward the church. He figured the person leaving was Gear Junkie, and he would have called out to him but he didn't want to wake Streaming.

"It wasn't me," Gear Junkie insisted. "Whoever you thought you heard was someone else. I left almost immediately after you fell asleep, and besides, I didn't run. I was extra quiet because I didn't want to wake Growler."

"My goodness, you boys are certainly considerate," chuckled Alain.

"Well, then I guess I was mistaken. Maybe it was Growler I heard. I wonder what he was doing?"

"I can't imagine," said Gear Junkie. "Maybe he was running away after he stole your money."

Will was staring at the rain and didn't respond.

Alain broke the silence. "Tracker, is there something you don't want to tell us?"

Will squirmed. After a minute, he spoke. "Okay. I confess. I haven't been completely honest." His delivery was deadpan, and Alain and Gear Junkie sat up to hear the revelation.

"All those noises up there gave me the creeps, and I got a little scared, so I came down to stay at the hostel."

"How did you get a room? They told me there were no vacancies."

"When I didn't find an empty bed, I slept out here." He paused before looking back up at them and burst out laughing.

"Man, you scared me," chided Gear Junkie. "For a minute there, you had me believing you were the killer. I was serious about Growler taking your money, though. You weren't there this morning to see him drop a big wad of cash on the floor."

"Really? And after I bought him dinner and everything."

Alain coughed.

"Oh, sorry Mr. Apple. I meant after I *offered* to buy him dinner."

"Hey, what if Streaming took it?" Gear Junkie asked. "He

could have faked snoring the whole time. What if he waited until I left and then stole it? That could have happened."

"I doubt Streaming took your money," said Alain. "He seemed an honorable young man to me. I picked up some news today that he went to the police last night around nine o'clock. He must have slipped away when he walked me out of The White Horse."

"But Streaming told us he was going this morning," said Will. "I wonder why he changed his mind and went last night?"

Gear Junkie was just as surprised. "How did you find out he went to the cops, Mr. Apple?"

"A small town has as many eyes as a fly."

"Ha ha, what a cool expression. Is it original?"

"I wish I could say so, but it's from a short story by a friend of mine. But I digress. Seriously, I ran into Ranger Cody today, and he told me."

Will interrupted. "Now that I think about it, Streaming was gone from the table a long time."

Alain continued, "He suggested to the police that the victim from the shelter might be this Red Rover person, and he volunteered to identify him. Cody showed him a bunch of Polaroids from the albums in the Hiker Lounge. Even with the names redacted, he picked out Red Rover right away."

"What do you mean he picked him out? Becky told us the victim was a local guy. That doesn't sound like Red Rover," said Gear Junkie.

"You're right, it didn't. By identifying Red Rover in the photograph, what he did was rule Red Rover out as the victim. Cody told me the dead body looked nothing like him."

"Well, that's a relief!" Gear Junkie said. "Now if only we knew who got killed last night."

"Does the name Patrick Myers ring a bell with any of you?" asked Alain. "The bed you'll be sleeping in tonight was supposed to be his. I learned his name when I peeked at the registration sheet while we were standing at the counter at check-in earlier. According to the authorities, it's also the name of the unfortunate young man found dead this morning."

"I don't recognize that name, but somebody must have met him."

"I'm afraid we all knew him," said Alain. "By his trail name, Streaming. And he couldn't have stolen your money, Tracker, because they found no money on him."

Gear Junkie's eyes watered, and he turned away from Alain for a moment of private grief.

"I know, son," said Alain, giving him a pat on his shoulder. "He was a good man. I'm so sorry."

Their intimate exchange was interrupted when Moonbeam sloshed on the porch. On the way back from the police station, she got caught in the downpour and was soaked. The colors of her hand-painted hair dripped down her cheeks and mixed with tears.

"I don't know what to do," she moaned. "Hardware's leaving. I rented out my apartment for two months, so now I've got nowhere to live. What with some lunatic killing people and bears running around, hiking is out of the question. And just when everything was turning around for me."

She unloaded her tragic story. A few weeks earlier Moonbeam met a guy at a neighborhood bar in Hoboken. She liked his free spirit and not minding that she paid for his drinks. After two passionate days and nights together at her apartment, he became edgy. He was between jobs, short on cash, and needed a complete change of scene so he could get back on his feet. Moonbeam told him she had the solution.

She was so fascinated with her role following Will's hike, she'd done some research of her own about the Appalachian Trail. Camping under the stars sounded romantic, and she talked her new boyfriend into sharing the adventure. He told her it sounded like a dream and hoped they could leave as soon as possible. Within two days, she invested in equipment and train tickets, and they were on a train headed for Harpers Ferry.

The night before they were to start their hike, the boyfriend excused himself from the dinner table to use the men's room and never came back. After twenty minutes and fearing the worst, she banged on the door. Where there was no answer, she screamed his name, which drew the attention of a young man at the bar. He introduced himself as Hardware and informed her that he'd witnessed the gentleman she described rushing out the back door. The shock of being jilted passed quickly when Hardware offered to buy her a drink. Not only did he provide the immediate comfort she needed, he seemed willing and able to take the relationship a step further in her bed at the hostel.

"He loved the romance of disappearing together for a while on the trail, and since I already had everything we needed, he told me it was a sign. But now after our special time together, he tells me he's suddenly been called back to Berlin." Hardware emerged from the hostel and took a seat with the others. "Speak of the devil. He's leaving as soon as he can get a flight. I'm so depressed, I don't know what I'm going to do."

"Business," Hardware said, nodding and frowning.

"I hate to spoil your travel plans," said Alain. "But since you and Moonbeam discovered the body, I would imagine it might be quite some time before the authorities will allow you to leave the country, or even Harpers Ferry, for that matter."

"Now I wish we'd gone to work at the farm with the rest of you," she lamented. "Everything would have been so much better."

"It's not too late," said Alain. "The farm you all are talking about is technically within the town's jurisdiction. You'll be safe there. I'll take you myself. In fact, we can all go in my truck."

"But what about the rain?" asked Moonbeam. "I don't want to have to camp in this terrible weather."

"I wouldn't be too concerned about that," said Alain. "I

suspect they'll put you up in their bunkhouse. I understand it's quite nice."

"Let's go, then. The sooner, the better. It's dangerous around here!" said Will, jumping to his feet. "I'll run and get my stuff."

"Not so fast!" came an authoritative voice from the side of the porch. It was Ranger Cody.

"Oh, excuse me, Mr. Apple. I'm sorry for the bother, but I have a warrant here for the arrest of a hiker known as Tracker. I'm afraid he's a suspect in our murder investigation."

Alain looked as stunned as the others. "Cody, there must be some mistake. I know this young man, and I'm certain he..."

Will stepped forward. "I'm Tracker." He stood straight and appeared calm, but his confident façade took a hit when his voice cracked. "I'm innocent, and I've got nothing to hide."

As he read him his rights, Cody slapped him in handcuffs.

"Are those necessary?" asked Alain.

"Sorry, Mr. Apple. Tracker, you're being charged with the murder of a man at the Shady Pines shelter."

The hikers gasped, and Alain looked shaken. "Tracker, can this be true?"

Ranger Cody continued. "And also for the murder of Patrick Myers, found dead at Jefferson Rock."

Gear Junkie followed him out to the squad car. "Tracker, tell me he's making a mistake!"

"I can explain everything," Will yelled, as the door to the car slammed shut.

Chapter 24

lvaro banged on the outhouse door. There was no
response and this time he kicked at the door. Growler
was groggy and poked out his head, and when Alvaro
announced he was taking Growler to the farmhouse for dinner,
Growler didn't understand. He unlocked the door anyway and
waddled out. He was in a vile mood and he smelled horrible.

The wind and rain lashed with a fury until late in the afternoon, and Growler's tent had filled with water. Completely
soaked, at some point he shimmied out backward and wobbled
to the latrine. He figured as horrible as it sounded, waiting out
the rain in the tiny shack would be his best chance at drying
out. The outhouse was worse than he imagined. The roof was
too low for him to stand, and there was not enough space on the
filthy floor for him to sit, even if he wanted to give it a try.
Consequently, he spent the afternoon sitting upright on the
wooden outhouse seat. The sound of rain pelting the tin roof
gradually made him drowsy, but the powerful stench stuck in
his nostrils, making him tense and preventing him from relaxing. Eventually, it was too much, and he collapsed against one of
the walls and fell asleep.

"Where have you been?" he shouted at Alvaro, waving his

hands. "They said meals were included. Me hungry!" Shaking his head, Alvaro shook his head and gestured for him to hop on his golf cart. On the way to the house, they made a stop at the barn, where Lana Lang lounged on a hay bale, eating a banana and texting.

Growler was furious. He jumped off the cart and stormed over, and for a second time his bullying behavior was a flop. His shoes were so thoroughly soaked, they made comic squishing sounds with every step, and Lana Lang looked more amused than intimidated. "How come you got special treatment? And where did you get that banana?"

Without looking up, she flicked off three pieces of loose hay from her dry clothes. "Special treatment? What are you talking about? For the record, the banana is mine because I thought to bring my own food." She bit off the last piece and chewed it slowly for his benefit.

Suddenly, Tornado, Einstein, and Shoe Store appeared from the bunkhouse door. All three were drinking beer and laughing. Einstein apologized for being late. "Hope I didn't keep you waiting too long. The shower had great water pressure, and I stayed under it as long as I could stand it."

"Hold on! You stayed here, too? How come nobody told me about all this?" He glared at Lana Lang.

"Don't look at me, Marion. When he showed us where to pitch our tents, Alvaro told us both a storm was expected, and that we could stay here in the bunkhouse if we wanted. I moved in as soon as the rain started. On my way, I noticed you were still in your tent, so I assumed you wanted to stay there. God, why do you smell like crap?"

Growler was pissed that she conveniently chose not to translate that important offer. Since nobody wanted to sit next to him in the cart, Alvaro instructed him to use the drop-down seat in the back. The giant yellow and white striped tent dominated the lush grassy farmhouse lawn, and as the silent electric golf cart neared, they could hear people on the inside holding conversations. When Alvaro opened the side flap, they were astonished to find Gear Junkie, Moonbeam, and Hardware standing together in a cluster, sampling hors d'oeuvres and sipping wine.

"How did you all get here?" asked Growler, surveying the spread. "And who do I have to see around here for a brewski?"

While Moonbeam explained how they arrived in Mr. Apple's truck, Alvaro reappeared with a silver tray bearing a cut-crystal glass of wine for each of them.

The incongruity of silver and stemware at a picnic was understandably perplexing. "Whose farm is this, anyway?" Lana Lang asked. A tinkle of a spoon against a goblet led to the answer.

"Ladies and gentlemen," said Alvaro in perfect English, pulling back a flap at the end of the tent. "Your host, Señor Apple."

Alain de la Pomme entered with a flourish. "Welcome, welcome."

THERE WERE gasps and double-takes from the guests. Gone was the cheap wig. His silver hair was long and thick and gathered into a ponytail. A black Barbour wool cardigan sweater, open at the collar, framed the perfect Windsor knot of a fashionably skinny gray necktie, which was stunning against a pristine starched white shirt. He wore tailored gray wool slacks, and in defiance of the soggy ground, highly polished Italian loafers. Alain chuckled to think how little he resembled the Mr. Apple they met the night before.

"I'm so glad everyone could join me here at my home," he said with a twinkle.

At Mr. Apple's signal, Alvaro moved the group to the dining

table set in the middle of the tent. A place card at each seat bore their trail names, and the hikers circled the large round table to find their places. One of the cards surprised Gear Junkie. "Dr. Apple?"

"Yes, Gear Junkie. I may have forgotten to mention my stint in graduate school."

Alain refilled each of their glasses. "I think a nice Côtes du Rhône is perfect at a picnic, don't you?" He winked at Lana Lang. "I like mine served at about eighteen degrees Centigrade." Before they sat down, he asked everyone to raise their glasses in a silent toast to their absent friend, Streaming.

"Why do we have to toast him?" Lana Lang griped. "He's not even here."

Alain pretended to be surprised. "Oh, of course. You couldn't possibly know." He took a few minutes to report the sad news of Streaming, known to the rest of the world as Patrick Myers.

"Was it the bears?" asked Tornado. "It was only a matter of time before they would attack again."

"No. Worse," said Alain. "Murdered. And I can't imagine why."

"I just remembered something that's giving me the creeps," said Gear Junkie. "Last night when we were up at the lookout, Tracker tried to talk us into staying there for the night, and this is the strange part. I remember Streaming say he had no intention of waking up at Jefferson Rock. It's like he knew something."

"Well, he got his wish, didn't he?" said Lana Lang. Then looking remorseful, she changed her tone. "Do they know who killed him?"

"Yes, I'm afraid so. This afternoon they arrested Tracker for both murders," said Alain. "It shocked us all. Tracker seemed like such a nice young man and so well-mannered. To think he was a murderer all along."

The hikers exchanged nervous glances, but Gear Junkie

spoke up first. "Look, it's got to be a mistake. We all knew Tracker. He wouldn't hurt a fly. Besides, he told me he was innocent."

Moonbeam had a theory. "Call it a woman's intuition if you like, but I believe Tracker is one of those, um, people you read about every once in a while. People who lead two separate lives. Um, there's the person you think you know, and then you find out there's, hm, a whole side of them you knew nothing about. What do you think, Lana Lang? You're a woman like me."

Lana Lang rolled her eyes. "Well, let's get one thing straight. First, I'm not a woman like you. And I don't want to talk about Tracker. He wasn't my type, either, a bit goody-goody for my taste."

"How can you say goody-goody? I mean, um, he murdered someone."

"Sorry. I just don't believe it," said Gear Junkie.

"Don't believe what?" Growler had only been paying half attention to the conversation. He was starving and preoccupied combining single burgers into doubles. He slathered his super-sized portions with mustard and ketchup. "These are very good. What's your secret, Dr. Apple?"

"No big secret. They're veggie burgers."

"Really? I wish you hadn't told me. But still, they're not half bad." Growler repeated his question to Gear Junkie.

"I said I don't believe that Tracker killed Streaming. It doesn't make any sense."

"Yeah, cops don't run in perps for no reason. Besides, if he killed Streaming, it wouldn't be a stretch to assume he killed the other guy, too, wouldn't you think?"

"Like I told you, I didn't like him, but I think they got the wrong guy," said Lana Lang. She pointed at Growler. "I still believe you are the killer. I always did."

"Me? Why me?" he stuttered.

"Because everything about you is suspicious, all the lies, slipping out the back door of the restaurant to run from the cops."

"The expensive backpack and jacket," interjected Gear Junkie.

"Your hands," said Moonbeam, joining in the pile on.

"Hey, lay off! They didn't arrest me, did they? It was Tracker they wanted,"

Gear Junkie waved to break off the argument and get Growler's attention. "Hey. You said you were going to sleep in the church ruins last night. Tracker said he heard you running down the steps in the middle of the night. Did you leave? And did you notice if Streaming was asleep when you did?"

"It wasn't me. Anyway, how would I know if Streaming was sleeping or not? I never stayed in that old church. It was too spooky, and I went somewhere else to crash."

"What are you talking about, Growler? It's lies like this that make everyone suspect you. We know you were there," said Moonbeam, giving a side-eye to Hardware. She pinched her nose and made a disgusting face. "We found your, um, evidence all over the place."

"What do you mean by evidence?"

"Your poop," said Hardware. "I scooped it up, and it vas all over da place."

Moonbeam pulled his scarf from her bag. "We found this in there, too."

Alain intervened. "Growler is quite right. The police didn't arrest him, so they must not believe his is guilty, and I'm certainly not going to let you put him on trial here at my picnic. But considering these unsettling circumstances, I hope you all will feel free to stay here for as long as you like. And that goes for your boyfriend, too, Lana Lang. When he gets to town, he's welcome to join us out here. I want to do everything I can to keep everyone safe and sound."

"Well, if there is a murderer among us, as you say, I don't feel safe or sound," she snorted. "And my boyfriend won't be joining me here, either, thank you very much, because I'm leaving." She slid her chair back from the table.

She made the prospect of getting on the trail and out of the area sound appealing, and Tornado was the first to agree. "The guys and I have been talking. We want to leave, too. We packed our stuff, and we're ready to go whenever you are."

"If you're leaving, I'm going too," said Growler. He turned to Mr. Apple. "Um, are we still going to get paid?"

"For what?" laughed Alain. He gestured to Alvaro. "Please run them back to Harpers Ferry now, will you?"

"I'd be happy to," he replied.

"You mean that guy spoke English the whole time?"

"I speak five languages," Alvaro said, placing another plate of burgers on the table.

Growler grabbed two. "Dr. Apple, do you mind if I take a couple of these with me for the road tonight?"

"Take what you like. Just make sure you all have your IDs handy. The authorities are mounting a huge manhunt, and they're checking everyone, and I mean everyone. Both coming and going."

"What for?" asked Lana Lang. "They've arrested the killer, so the case should be closed."

"Oh, no. The manhunt I'm talking about is the search for William François Chillon de la Pomme. Apparently, he is still missing."

"How could he be?" she asked. "Isn't he the French guy they said was dead? I thought you just told us they pinned his murder on Tracker, too."

"They pinned the murder of the guy at the shelter on him, but it wasn't Mr. de la Pomme."

"Mr. Apple is right!" said Gear Junkie. "It was someone else. Becky at The Beanery told me it was some local guy."

"Who's Becky?" asked Growler.

"She's the waitperson you stiffed," said Gear Junkie.

Lana Lang shook her head. "How come a dumb waitress knows more than the cops?" she grumbled. "So, that means he's still around here somewhere, too, doesn't it?"

"That's what I've been saying," said Gear Junkie.

"Well, I couldn't care less. I'm taking my chances on foot." She looked peeved. "That way I won't have to screw around with a bunch of bureaucrats and checkpoints."

"Good idea. You won't have to endure all that red tape," said Alain. The idea of producing an ID seemed to make her nervous, and he wanted to learn why. They couldn't all be murderers.

Hardware didn't want to put up with delays, either, and he announced he would take his chances with Lana Lang, reminding everyone he had a plane to catch. He gave Moonbeam a peck on the cheek. "You don't mind if I go with Lana Lang, do you?"

Moonbeam clutched his hand. "If you're leaving, I'm going with you, at least as far as the airport." She glared at Lana Lang, then at Hardware. "I don't know, baby. Maybe I'll fly to Berlin with you, too."

"Who said I was going to Berlin?"

Flashing lights announced the arrival of a police car, and when the car door slammed, Growler leaped to his feet. "I've got to use the bathroom!" he lied. Spilling his wine and knocking over his chair, he dashed out of the tent.

The side flap opened, and Will sauntered in. "Hey, is there any dinner left?" His triumphant grin was so wide, his silver capped tooth sparkled as he yelled to the other side of the tent. "You can come back in, Growler. It's only me, Tracker!"

"What about the murder rap?" asked Growler, taking his place at the table again. "How did you beat that?"

"Some junior level person bungled the paperwork. Turns out I wasn't a suspect. It was all a big mistake."

Gear Junkie raised his glass to make a toast to Tracker, when suddenly he stopped mid-sentence. "Wait a minute! Dr. Apple, didn't you tell me that the authorities had rounded up everyone on the trail and they're all here?"

"Everyone for miles around."

"So, if the body at the shelter wasn't him, that means the billionaire is one of us, doesn't it?"

"That's right," said Will. "And another one is the real killer."

Chapter 25

Alain didn't have to ask his stunned guests. The revelation that both de la Pomme and the assassin were among them called for more wine.

Moonbeam's eyes bulged. "If the murderer is here, why are the rest of us sitting around? Shouldn't someone call the police?"

"Don't worry. Even the dumbest killer wouldn't try anything in a room full of people. You're safe for now." Alain excused himself and returned a moment later with earbuds draped down his shoulders. They connected to a small metal gadget he held in his hands.

"Does anybody recognize this?" His question was met with blank stares. "Never mind. I'll demonstrate."

Lana Lang crossed her arms. "I'm not the least bit interested. I think I'll pass."

"Actually, Lana Lang. You all have to stay."

"Says who? Are you a cop or something?"

"Not exactly." Alain saw the alarm in their eyes, but he noticed that nobody got up to leave. He always counted on his charisma to command a room, and he was pleased he hadn't lost his touch.

"Well, I hope you're not going to give a long speech."

"Then I'd better get right down to business, hadn't I?" He turned from her and held up the device. "This thing works something like a Geiger counter, but instead of recognizing metal, it detects something that emits a different frequency. Before I turn the thing on, I'd like to introduce someone in the room who understands the underlying technology." He looked at each face around the table.

Gear Junkie was the first to respond. "One of us?"

"Yes." Alain spun around and handed the object to Alvaro.

"Are you kidding me?" Growler shook his head and looked at the others for solidarity. "Him again? Why?"

"Because Dr. Cortes can explain it better than I can."

Alvaro spoke slowly and in flawless English, but at any speed the arcane programming jargon was foreign to most, and their glazed eyes showed he was losing his audience.

"I still don't understand a word he says," complained Growler. "Even when he's speaking English."

"Does anyone else know what he's talking about?" asked Moonbeam. "I'm with Growler. I'm not following him."

"Dr. Cortes may have forgotten to tell you that computer code is one of his five languages," said Alain. "I'm sorry if it's over your head."

"What he's talking about is basic YavaScript," interjected Hardware.

"Well, can someone translate for us dummies?" snickered Gear Junkie.

Alain agreed the technology was complex, and he agreed to dumb it down. He explained the gadget picked up certain frequencies emitted by specific objects, in this case, the labels embedded in the clothing and gear belonging to the missing hiker.

"William de la Pomme. I knew it," exclaimed Gear Junkie. "The newspaper said they sewed GeoFibre labels in his equipment and clothing. But why would anyone need to find his stuff? Wouldn't he still have his gear with him?"

Alain acknowledged Gear Junkie was right. They were talking about the billionaire. Some of his things had been stolen from him, and the authorities planned to scan the belongings of every hiker in Harpers Ferry until they found everything, starting with the hikers staying at Alain de la Pomme's farm.

Lana Lang perked up. "With all the dead bodies piling up around here, why are the police concerned with something as minor as a little stolen property?"

"I'm afraid the situation is more complicated than that," Alain said. "Before he died, Streaming gave Ranger Cody other information they tell me was very helpful."

"Streaming actually went to the police? When?"

"Last night, around nine o'clock."

"He was away from the table for a long time," said Gear Junkie. "That must have been when he went to talk to them."

"Well, I wish he'd told me," griped Lana Lang. "I wasted all that time waiting around for him this morning."

"Streaming's dead, and you're complaining about an inconvenience?"

Alain turned on the scanner. Even from across the room the beeps through the earbuds were loud enough for everyone at the table to hear. The closer he got, the louder and faster came the beeps. He aimed the gadget in Will's direction, and the noise stopped. When he turned to Growler's jacket and backpack, loud beeps blurred into a steady screech.

"I told you he was a criminal!" yelled Lana Lang. "This proves he stole those things from the dead French dude." She held up her cellphone and the screenshot of Growler. "And I've got more proof. Look! 'Marion Agronsky a.k.a. Bad Boy Bill a.k.a Big Tony.' He's running from a hit and run charge. His picture is all over the Internet."

"That's fake news. I'll kill you for this!" Growler lunged at her.

In a surprising move, Hardware jumped in front of Lana Lang and shoved Growler to the ground.

"See? What did I tell you?" she blared. "Keep me away from him. He's dangerous."

"So romantic of Hardware to protect you," said Alain. "You make a good couple."

Before Lana Lang had time to protest, Moonbeam exploded, "What do you mean a couple? Him with her? You must be joking."

"Oh, you weren't aware? Streaming saw them together. Please don't make me describe what he said they were doing."

Moonbeam put her head in her hands and screamed, but Gear Junkie made her stop. "Can we please focus here? A few minutes ago, Growler tried to kill Lana Lang!"

"She made me. That woman was always out for me," shouted Growler. "I didn't off anybody!"

"I suppose you didn't take my money, either, did you?" Tracker asked.

"Of course not." Growler's face paled.

"Perhaps you could explain to Tracker why his money clip fell out of your pocket when you dropped all that cash at The Beanery," said Alain.

"Well, yeah, I took your stupid money. But here, you can have it back!" He fished around his pocket and tossed the stack of crumpled bills on the table. "Look. Lifting a little dough doesn't make me a murderer! Anyway, last time I saw Streaming, he was sleeping over in that rock."

Will and Gear Junkie exchanged panicked looks, and Will said, "That wasn't Streaming sleeping. You were looking at his dead body."

"You mean the killer walked right by me? I could have been attacked! Now do you believe I'm not the murderer?"

Alain stepped in. "No one is accusing you of killing anyone, Growler. But I want to know how you ended up with young Mr. de la Pomme's gear. Did he give it to you?"

"Yes. He did." Growler looked at their reactions to gauge his response. "One hundred percent he did."

Dr. Cortes plopped Growler's cheap daypack on the table. "Would you like to change your story?"

As Growler sputtered the beginnings of a denial, Alain produced the receipt for the pack and everything else he bought that day in the big box store. "How did you get that?"

Once they had his fingerprints, Marion Agronsky's tracks were easy to trace, and his story was simple to disprove. He had made such a bad impression, that the clerk was more than happy to tell the police about the entire insulting encounter. He paid for everything with a stolen credit card.

"It might help, Growler, if you told us how you ended up with Red Rover's gear," said Alain.

Growler shifted in his chair. "Okay, look. So, when I got to Shady Pines the other night, a guy was sitting on a log facing the campfire. The fire was almost burned out, but it put out enough light that I could see he was slumped over. He looked like he was sleeping. I didn't want to scare him, you know, by like suddenly coming up from behind, so I called across the clearing."

When Growler's stomach rumbled, he remembered being surprised that the noise didn't wake him up. He quietly set a log on the fire. It was then he noticed the pot of noodles. He was starving and convinced the man was sound asleep, so he helped himself.

"I told him he was a darned good cook. I knew he was sleeping, but at the time, I thought my one-way conversation was funny."

Lana Lang sent Growler a nasty stare. "So, you complimented the guy and then killed him for his food and his backpack?"

"No! I keep telling you, I didn't kill anyone."

He planned to eat the rest of the food and scram before the guy woke up. But when he brushed against him as he reached to grab his canteen, the guy teetered to the ground.

"It wasn't until I heard about them finding the body at the shelter, I put two and two together and figured out he was dead when I got there."

"Now we know he can add," mumbled Lana Lang.

"Since nobody else was around, I thought I might as well finish off the rest of the noodles. Like I said, I hadn't eaten for a day or two."

"Yeah, the last time was probably when you bummed a meal off me," said Tornado. "I remember your sad story about animals eating your food, or people stealing your pots and pans, or something. I didn't believe you then, either."

"You didn't?" He gulped his wine. "Well, I was telling the truth. I was lucky those bears didn't eat me alive."

Alain refilled his glass and snickered. "Yes, yes. Your recollection sounds terrifying. But we still want you to tell us how you got Mr. de la Pomme's things."

"I was still cold, and the kid in the store sold me a cheap piece of crap jacket."

The coat Growler bought hadn't kept him warm or dry. The guy on the ground was about his size, and his jacket was heavier than Growler's. He was slipping off the guy's insulated long-sleeved t-shirt when he spotted the green backpack. He picked that up, too. He didn't have to bother checking out the contents. He could tell the new backpack looked better than his.

"So, you ripped off both his backpack and his coat. What a creep!" said Gear Junkie.

"Look. I was trying to survive. Besides, I covered him with the tarp. Anyway, I let him keep his cooking stuff and his tent!" He was about to leave, when he felt bad for the guy. He threw the body over his shoulder fireman-style and laid him on the sleeping platform.

"Ick." Moonbeam stuck her fingers in her ears. "This is too weird for one day."

"I remember thinking he must have been a heavy sleeper. His head kept flopping and banging on my back every time I took a step, and he still didn't wake up. But getting him out of the cold was the least I could do."

"A heavy sleeper? He was dead." Alain held up the daypack. "So, I guess you left this flimsy thing with him."

"Was this the trade you told us about?" asked Will.

"Why would anyone believe a word Growler says?" Lana Lang turned to Alain. "Sir, the man you are looking for is sitting right in front of you. Are you going to arrest him or not?"

"Oh, I'm not a cop. Merely a concerned citizen. And Dr. Cortes here is a talented programmer. No, we aren't here to arrest anyone. But Growler, you should hand over the things you stole so we can return them to Ranger Cody."

"How am I supposed to hike the trail without a backpack or any of my stuff?"

"Your stuff?" sighed Gear Junkie.

"There are often useful items in the Swap Box," joked Dr. Cortes. "You'll find it along the back wall of the Hiker Lounge."

Alain said there was still another item they were looking for, and he reactivated the scanner. He pointed the thing first at Hardware and next at Moonbeam. The crackling sound fell off and remained equally quiet when he aimed it at Tornado and the other two hikers.

"How about seeing what it does with Gear Junkie?" asked Growler. "He's the one who's so interested in hiking gear."

When he turned the scanner back past Hardware and Moonbeam and directed it at Gear Junkie, Gear Junkie asked why everyone was so surprised it didn't make a peep. "I hope you don't believe I could steal anyone's gear. It would be a sacrilege."

The scanner squawked again when he pointed it at the remaining person in the room, Lana Lang. "What? Me? What the hell is going on?" she barked. "That dumb thing must be on the fritz."

Growler laughed at her predicament and suggested maybe she was the thief and the killer. Alan, meanwhile, announced the scanner was picking up William de la Pomme's label in her sweater.

"Looks like a man's sweater to me. It's definitely wool, but I confess, I don't know the brand," said Gear Junkie.

"Nice guess, genius. I told you in the restaurant I like to wear my boyfriend's clothes."

Moonbeam came to her defense. "I wear men's sweatshirts all the time. They make my chest stand out. These, um, tits of mine have always driven men crazy. Sometimes, um, they can be a real curse. Lana Lang, I think you understand."

Lana Lang reached down and peeled off her sweater, revealing a long-sleeved insulated t-shirt. "No, um, as you can see, um, I don't know what you mean. Here!" She tossed the sweater to Alain, who caught it in the air. "Like I said, I got it from my boyfriend." She got to her feet. "I'm tired of all the insinuations and character assassinations. I don't care if there are rangers or not. I'm getting out of here. I can sneak past them in the dark."

"Well, then, I'm leaving, too," announced Growler, stuffing his pockets with burgers and everything else he could scavenge from the table.

One by one, they agreed to leave under the cover of dark. Even Tracker decided he wanted a change of scenery, after all the drama that surrounded him in Harpers Ferry.

Alain stood. "If that's what you all want to do, I'm happy to help. There is a spot where you can enter the trail and disappear in no time. And Lana Lang is right. The visitors will all be gone, and I doubt anyone will notice you in the dark. Pack up your gear, and I'll take you there. We'll leave in twenty minutes."

WHILE THE HIKERS rushed to gather their things, Alain initiated a video call with Suzen. Before she joined, Will turned to his uncle, and suddenly his face fell.

"I can't stop thinking about Streaming. I'm not sure why I thought I could handle things up there by myself, and I wish I hadn't talked you into letting me try."

"Streaming's death was not an accident, Will. Someone wanted him dead and would see to it one way or another."

"I've always been too trusting of people. I had no clue Growler would try to push me off the rock. Maybe it wasn't intentional. But I showed him my money like you suggested, and perhaps it was too irresistible for him. He saw Gear Junkie leave to take a leak, and maybe he thought he could convince people I slipped off by myself while he wasn't looking."

"I think you're right. Growler's a mystery. With his record, he's an obvious suspect. He's amoral, too, but I just can't help thinking he's not smart enough to be our guy."

Suzen's video stream joined their group chat.

"Just in time," said Alain. "We're getting close to naming our killer."

Suzen was confused. "What makes you so sure? A while ago you weren't convinced you had all the suspects, and I'm starting to think you're right. Going over the list makes me wonder if we missed another hiker or two in the drone sweep."

"You mean like Lana Lang's fictional boyfriend?" teased Alain.

"Oh, I don't think that's so far-fetched. I know she's always snapping at Growler, but who wouldn't? She seems to like me," said Will.

"Well, I have a theory about the boyfriend, and I'll run it past you soon."

In the meantime, Suzen wanted to review the narrowing list of suspects. Gear Junkie was at the bottom of the list, and he seemed as squeaky clean as his fingerprints, but there was still his obsession with Will and GeoFibre. Though he couldn't imagine a motive, Alain suggested it still could be a ploy to get closer. Tornado reported that there was still nothing about either of his two hikers that was the least bit suspicious.

"Growler's good at manipulation, Suzen, and I'm putting him back up near the top of my list."

"Okay, but if he's so masterful, why did he allow himself to get caught for those petty crimes? I can't begin to understand your business, Alain, but if Growler had just committed a hit and run, and we know he did, I don't see why he would further complicate things by committing a murder."

"That's a good point. Look, up to now I've wanted him to look guilty, to let the real culprit make a mistake. And if he's not the killer, when the time comes, we'll bring him in on the other charges."

"You said you put him near the top. Who do you have as number one?"

"First, let me tell you what I think happened at the shelter." He explained that the local boy who someone killed was probably out looking to roll a hiker, maybe steal a new coat. That he got wind of a hiker named Red Rover with expensive taste and figured he was probably carrying some cash, too.

"I doubt that guy intended to kill anybody. He just ended up being at the right place at the wrong time," said Will.

Le Mauvais somehow learned that Will was wearing trackable gear and would have built the gizmo Alain found to locate him by the labels. The guy was wearing Will's coat, and because the scanner was probably beeping like crazy, he killed him, thinking he was Will. According to the logs, they learned the sweater and the watch were the first items to leave the campsite, so it made sense that the killer took them. The speed they left would be consistent with someone who was fleeing a crime scene.

"Lana Lang was wearing my sweater, but she insisted her boyfriend gave it to her. Since Streaming saw her with Hardware on the trail, we could make a case that Hardware is really her boyfriend, and that he killed the guy, stole his sweater, and gave it to her."

"Whew, I'm confused," said Suzen. "So, is Hardware our killer?"

"Looks that way to me," said Alain.

"My gosh. I bet Lana Lang and Moonbeam have no idea how dangerous he is. We've got to keep a protective eye on them."

Suzen was still confused about the strategy of dropping off everyone in town. "Aren't you running the risk of letting the assassin get away? Whoever it is?"

"We've got that covered. Anyway, we're not just letting them out anywhere. We're dropping them off at the old Arsenal ruins. From there a footpath leads across a quarter-mile-long railroad bridge that crosses the Potomac River into Maryland. Once they enter the bridge, they'll be contained until they reach the other side. If the assassin doesn't reveal himself by the time the group reaches the other end, they will all be picked up and brought back in. Then we'll start all over."

"Before I forget, the guys told me they will have everything back online in about two hours. They apologized for how long it took, but the virus was elaborate. I'll let you know as soon as it's up."

"That's good, Suzen, and please thank them for all the work they put in. As you know, we've already located all of Will's things. How some of it got to each person is still a mystery I hope to solve when our system is back in service."

There were murmurs and paper shuffling on the other end of the line. "Great news, Alain. I just got the MP4 from the security footage we've been waiting for. I just took a quick glance, and I think you will be pleased. Maybe not surprised, though. I'm sending it to you now."

"Suzen, how can you keep us in suspense?" asked Will.

Alain's phone vibrated. He smiled as he watched the video clip of a man breaking into the GeoFibre server facility. Hardware's face and his multiple piercings were unmistakable.

Alain turned to share the screen with his team. "Ladies and gentlemen, meet our killer!"

Chapter 26

D r. Alvaro Cortes took many unnecessary turns as he drove the group in a circuitous route to the base of Washington Street. It was nearly midnight, and the town of Harpers Ferry was asleep when the truck pulled to the curb, and the hikers spilled out and onto the cobblestone street beside the ruins of the old Arsenal. He instructed them to take the path that led under the viaduct and follow the walkway, which would take them across the bridge. Once they got to the Maryland side of the river, they would find the entrance to the Appalachian Trail, and it would be easy to disappear.

The iron footbridge shared the span with active railroad tracks, and along with the regular train traffic, crossing the Potomac on the footbridge was popular with tourists and locals for the spectacular view of the two rivers that converged below.

Growler wasted no time, and he took off at the first opportunity.

"There he goes," said Gear Junkie, who watched him sprint around the others and onto the bridge. "Running away again. He just can't stop looking suspicious."

"What a loser!" snapped Lana Lang.

Two red lights marked the railroad tunnel on the Maryland

side of the bridge, and Growler used them as a guide and never looked back. At the other side, the train tracks and the footpath separated. The railroad headed straight ahead and into the tunnel, and the pedestrian section bent away to the right, where it stopped at the top of a broad circular iron stairway. Even in the dark, Growler could read the sign and the arrow pointing down for the C & O Canal.

He took one last look behind him, glad he'd outrun everyone. It felt good to be back in control again. As he started down the spiral staircase, he thanked his lucky stars he had extricated himself from yet another mess of his own creating. He didn't know where the canal or the Appalachian Trail would take him this time, and he didn't care. He would take their advice and disappear. Quickly. Maybe this time he'd settle in Philly. He knew some guys there who might set him up.

The iron stairway clanked under his shoes as he raced down the steps. The wind had picked up, and he was grateful for the railing. It was dark, and as he landed on the last step, he had to squint to make out the arrow on the small sign in front of him. He made the turn and followed the path a short distance where it passed by more crumbled brick ruins. The long sprint across the entire quarter mile of the bridge had left him breathless. His lungs were hurting and his heart was pounding. He was alone and decided he could afford to rest a few minutes. He closed his eyes.

"Raise those big hands of yours, sir, and don't try any funny stuff!"

Growler didn't recognize the woman's voice behind the stern warning, but when he felt the pistol jab into his back, he knew she meant business. He jerked his head around. Sergeant Rebecca "Becky" Wilson looked a lot different in her police uniform than she did in her wait staff apron pouring coffee at the café, but Growler recognized her. With a fluid motion that came only with years of practice, she slapped on the handcuffs and read him his rights.

"From the look of things, you've been a very busy man!" she said, as another officer took him into custody and led him away.

MOONBEAM AND HARDWARE were still arguing at the truck. He wanted to go on alone, and she begged him to take her with him. Each time he tried to leave, she tugged his arm. While she seemed heartbroken, Hardware remained insistent and dispassionate.

"You've changed," she wailed.

"You're a whiny little bitch."

Lana Lang looked impatient as she watched their spat from her position against the hood of the truck. "If you're still coming with me like we planned, you'd better come now because I'm leaving."

Moonbeam's heartache turned to rage, and she stormed over to Lana Lang. "This is all your fault!" she screamed. "You've been trying to steal him from the second you set eyes on him!"

"Oh, brother!" sighed Lana Lang. "I'm out of here." She picked up her gear, and following Alain's directions, she headed straight for the bridge, leaving the couple alone to resolve their problem.

"Ow, you're hurting me!" howled Moonbeam, as Hardware yanked his arm from her grip.

"I'm going with her!" he yelled. As he reached for his things, a voice made him stop.

"Not so fast, young man!" The demand came from the other side of the truck.

Hardware's eyes expressed his terror, but ignoring the request, he barreled past Moonbeam, knocking her to the ground. He grabbed for his gun but before he could draw it, someone tripped him. When he fell, his revolver skittered under the van and out of reach.

Agent Lucille "Lucky" Maguire presented a warrant for his arrest. "Search him," she ordered. Gone was the temporary tattoo encircling her forearm, and without her bleached blonde wig she no longer resembled the waitress from The White Horse. "Now!"

A second van materialized at the curb, and two agents shoved Hardware inside as they read him his rights. They searched his pockets.

"Well, look what I found, boss," one of them said. Laughing, he handed Alain the thumb drive. "I think he picked the wrong name. He should call himself 'Software.'"

"Or Le Mauvais," said Alain turning to Hardware. "After watching you slip through my hands all these years, seeing you helpless in my van is a dream come true."

"Who the hell are you?" shouted Hardware, waving his cuffed hands in the air.

"Don't play dumb with me." A glint of metal caught Alain's eye, and he remembered the watch. Finally, he had the chance to inspect it closely, and when he reached for it, Hardware squirmed.

"What's the matter, tough guy? Scared we're going to find it belongs to Mr. de la Pomme?"

"What are you talking about? I paid good money for this."

Since he wouldn't hand it over voluntarily, Alain instructed an agent to remove it from his wrist.

"Hey, take it easy!"

"And to think you were on my payroll," said Alain as the agent handed it over. It only took an instant in his hands for Alain to verify that Hardware was telling the truth. Though it was definitely top of the line, and from across the dinner table it bore a strong resemblance to Will's, Hardware's Epix was a different model. Surprised and embarrassed, Alain handed it back with a half-apology. "I don't know how you pulled that switch, Le Mauvais, but I'm not buying it. We'll charge him with the rest, later. So for now, book him on two counts of homicide."

"Are you crazy?" yelped Hardware, banging on the sides of the van. "I didn't kill anybody."

Chapter 27

Strong gusting crosswinds added to the turbulence and made it difficult to walk. Will, Lana Lang, and Gear Junkie were about a third of the way across the bridge when they stopped to wait for a break in the storm. The water level was high after the heavy rain, and a bright moon illuminated the raging rivers below. The power and majesty were too spectacular not to appreciate, and the three of them leaned against the railing in wonder.

The wind picked up again, and a strong gust whipped horizontally and caught the bill of Will's baseball cap. He grabbed for it as it loosened from his head, but he was too late. The hat and its fake black wig and ponytail flew up into the air, and the three of them watched the pieces sail out over the river. In the confusion, Gear Junkie had turned to face Tracker, and the transformation of the man who stood before him was astonishing.

"You're William de la Pomme!" he stammered. As if to verify his revelation, another gust of wind whipped around and swept through Will's thick head of auburn hair. "I can't believe I didn't recognize you."

Will had nothing to lose by telling the truth to Gear Junkie.

Now that they arrested the killer, they would soon go their separate ways.

"Yes, and there's a perfectly good reason for my disguise. I promise to tell you one of these days."

"So, Growler's backpack and jacket were yours, weren't they? I knew the odds of two people with that limited-edition pack were low."

Lana Lang became interested. "Does this mean you are the French guy everyone thought was dead?"

"No. Well, yes, but actually, I'm Swiss."

A woman screaming for help at the entrance to the bridge interrupted his clarification.

"Moonbeam!" shouted Gear Junkie. "She needs help!"

Without thinking, he and Will turned to run, but Lana Lang grabbed Will's arm, stopping him. "I'll take care of her," Gear Junkie yelled, as he sped back to the West Virginia side of the bridge.

"Oh, she's probably being dramatic again. I think Gear Junkie can handle that nut by himself." She turned and gave Will a big smile. "You have just become the most fascinating person on the planet, and I want to know everything about you."

Moonbeam was hysterical. "They arrested Hardware, and I need you to help me get him released!" she sputtered when Gear Junkie arrived. He was panting.

"Dr. Apple will know what to do. Where is he?"

The mention of Apple's name put her in a rage. "Mr. Apple? Are you joking? He's the one who had Hardware arrested!"

Alain was in the van when his phone vibrated. Suzen was calling with news that Will's tracking system would be back online at any moment.

"Not that it really matters, now, since he is safe with you, and you've arrested the killer. I'm sorry it took so long. Oh, and someone from Bangkok has been trying to reach you all evening. Said it was vitally important. Check your phone for his message."

Alain's face fell when he saw all the messages he'd gotten during the past couple of hours, including the multiple ones from his contact in Bangkok, all labeled URGENT. He clicked on the first one.

Forget Le Mauvais. It's La Mauvaise you want!

His mind raced. La Mauvaise. Thailand. Plastic surgery. Sex reassignment. Of course. Eighteen months in hiding was enough time for the transition. He had finally convinced everyone that Hardware was the killer, and all along it was Lana Lang. How did he miss all the clues? Suddenly, his blood froze.

"Wait! Where's Will?"

Alvaro pointed to the bridge. "He told me he was going to cross with everyone and would come right back."

"Get everyone back in their places," he yelled, as he raced across the bridge.

Will and Lana Lang were still staring at the churning water below and she was doing her best to show off her softer side. Her seduction started with a hand on the small of his back. Slowly it worked its way up, where her hand rested a moment before daring to rub his shoulders.

"They tell me I give a great massage," she cooed, as she moved to stand directly behind him. Fingers of both hands danced lightly over the nape of his neck. "You seem so tense. Is this helping?"

"Yes. Maybe up and over to the right a little." He closed his eyes and dropped his head as she found the spot and worked through the knots in his neck. The strength and thickness of her fingers surprised him, and he wondered why he hadn't noticed. He speculated it was because she nearly always wore her sweater sleeves pulled down over her wrists. But he didn't care. The opposing forces of the violent water below and the tenderness of her touch on his neck mesmerized him.

Her attention made him feel self-conscious, and he dealt with it the way he often did, with a joke. "You know, Lana Lang, I always thought you weren't as bitchy as that act you put on."

She was directly behind him now. *Men are so easy.* Revenge was close enough to taste.

At that precise instant, two hundred and sixty-five miles away on the twenty-seventh floor of the GeoFibre Foundation office in New York City, lights on the wall map twinkled back on as its computer booted back to life and instantly established a connection with a new controlling server operating from a secret location in Switzerland. One second later, Dillon, hair unwashed and eyes bloodshot from staring at the dashboard for twenty-four hours, saw the signal flash on the screen before him. He slammed on the Enter key.

The unbearably loud noise that screeched from Lana Lang's watch startled them both, and she lost her concentration. Hands poised to twist his neck knocked into Will's head instead. As she tried to recover her position and start over, Will spun around with time to catch her in the act.

Gone was any tenderness he felt earlier. He braced, and when she reached for his throat, he shoved her away. She came at him again, and he fended her off and knocked her down. Before she could scramble to her feet, Alain arrived and stood defiantly between her and Will.

"Well, well, well. Le Mauvais, I presume?"

"What? Who the hell are you?" she bristled.

"Ha! I'm the one you really want to kill."

She looked from Alain to Will and back to Alain, and she saw the resemblance. "You!" she growled. "That loser cop who could never catch me. It's about time you showed up."

"You almost fooled me again. I wasn't looking for a woman."

"You and your damn picture." She gestured to her face and torso. "You made me do all this."

"Well, I've got to hand it to you. You had excellent work

done. It's regrettable you didn't pay your Bangkok doctor what you owed him. He might not have squealed."

"He promised to make me look like Cate Blanchette, the hack."

"So, I have to ask. If this was about getting me, why did you try to kill my nephew?"

"Him? To give you a taste of your own medicine. Thanks to you, I had to leave my home. I never saw my wife and kids again, and they never knew why. Do you have any idea how devastating that was for them?" Her eyes darted as she assessed her exit options. "I knew if I killed your nephew, it would bring you here faster, and I could take you out, too."

"Too bad, you didn't get either of us. By the way, we've got your boyfriend, Hardware, back there. And I'm afraid you won't be seeing him for a long time."

"Don't be ridiculous. He's not my boyfriend, and it serves him right for getting caught. He was sloppy."

"Speaking of sloppy. I'd say you lost your touch. First, you kill the wrong man at the shelter, and then you leave your scanner at the fire for me to find."

"His fault, too. He said that piece of crap would make my job easier. I'm working alone again from now on."

"You're not going to work at all. I've got you this time." He pointed behind her. "You're trapped!"

Over her shoulder, Lucky charged toward her from behind. She flipped around and saw that Alvaro and Tornado had arrived and were blocking her way forward. "You're delusional," she smirked and turned to run in Lucky's direction. "I'll be back for you, later."

By the tilt of her body, Alain instinctively realized what she was about to do. "You'll never make it!"

He sprinted after her, and when she made a quick cut to the right, he stretched out a hand to grab her. But he overestimated his strength and speed and didn't get to her fast enough. She vaulted the railing as if it were a pommel horse and flung herself out into the pitch-black sky.

The others rushed to the railing in time to see her drop into the uncertain waters below. Seconds later, the powerful Potomac River swept up her body and discarded it into the turbulent currents of the confluence.

Chapter 28

LATER

Thanks to the proliferation of whitewater rafting centers along both the Shenandoah and Potomac rivers, there was no shortage of kayaks when Alain deployed his search and rescue team.

While the high-water level and resultant surge didn't carry Le Mauvais as far downstream as they calculated, she had a tough ride. Judging from the extensive punishment to her body and the known currents, river experts believe the Whitehorse Rapids near Bass Rock pummeled Lana Lang first before her wild ride took her past the Bird Sanctuary Islands via Miller's Hole. From there, they estimated she would have sailed on through toward the Weverton Gates Ruins had a submerged tree not slowed her down. Failing to grab one of its branches caused her to float several yards farther, where she would have ricocheted off a huge rock. Ultimately, her limbs got tangled up in a large vine that also encircled her neck.

The agency's pathologist determined the death was slow and tortuous. She would have struggled several hours in the strong current attempting to free herself from the same vine that eventually strangled her just off a small island known as Paradise.

"Strangled, how poetic." Suzen handed the autopsy report back to Alain.

"Gruesome is the term that comes to mind for me."

They were expecting Will and Gear Junkie to join them, but she arrived early. It was her first visit to his comfortable West Village home, and she was thrilled the distinctive building she passed by so often on her favorite street belonged to him. Alain served drinks in the sunlit living room on the parlor level, and he watched Suzen's jaw drop as she gazed at the high ceilings, fireplaces, and intricate detailing.

"I love your apartment," she said. "It's much more spacious than it appears from the outside."

"It's actually more than an apartment. I've got all four levels and the English basement. It's way more than I need, but I got a good deal on the whole house."

She made a mental note to check with a realtor friend about listings in the area. As the only other shareholder in GeoFibre, Suzen had profited mightily from the small but generous equity Will and Alain offered her early on, and she could afford something grander than her current apartment.

"I'm so glad you could come. You know, I haven't spent much time here in recent years, and I'm looking forward to doing this more often."

"You're sticking around in New York for a while, then?"

"I think so. At least half the time. I'd forgotten how much I like this neighborhood. Everything I need is only a block or two away. Besides, it gets lonely in Switzerland, and this way I'd get to be closer to everyone."

The guys arrived together. It was Gear Junkie's first visit to New York, and he'd been staying as Will's houseguest for a few days. Thanks to the generosity of the de la Pommes, he would finish his MBA as a full-time student and be leaving soon to return to Shepherdstown, West Virginia. In the meantime, Will had shown him the city in grand style.

"So, what do you think of our city?" asked Suzen. "Will said you two crammed in a lot."

"I love it. Then again, I love everywhere I go. I'm just as happy in the wilderness as I am in a big city. They're both equally dangerous."

"Equally less dangerous, now that a major assassin is out of commission," joked Alain.

"We were talking about Lana Lang's tortured demise, when you walked in," Suzen said. "Alain shared the autopsy with me. Have you read it, Will?"

"Not yet. I still feel foolish that I fell for her seduction act on the bridge."

"Hey, don't beat yourself up too much. By then everyone was certain that Hardware was Le Mauvais," she added.

"That's what I thought. After his arrest, I figured the case was closed. And it never occurred to me that Lana Lang was a threat. I didn't even worry when the wind whipped my hat off and blew my cover."

"Talk about thinking inside the box. I bought into her act, too," said Alain. "And I take the blame for never considering her a suspect. She had a convincing American accent, and her grammar was flawless, like many Europeans who learn English as children. I should have noticed the red flag she sent up when she admitted to not liking her beer cold. I assumed we were looking for a man, and that assumption clouded my thinking so much, I didn't even pull her fingerprints after we failed to get them the first time."

"It wouldn't have mattered. According to the autopsy, she'd had her fingerprints surgically removed," said Suzen. Without them, digging up personal information about her was impossible, until Hardware started singing to the authorities. They were both accomplished hackers and she met him in a murky corner of the dark web when she was a he and known to the world as Le Mauvais. When they discovered they shared the same sinister goals, Hardware agreed to help, and together they plotted revenge against Alain.

While she was transitioning in Thailand, it was Hardware's job to learn what he could about William de la Pomme. Getting hired at the GeoFibre lab turned out to be easy. He had an impeccable resumé, and they were always on the lookout for exceptional engineers. Once in the lab, he kept his head down and ears to the ground. He caught wind of Will's hike early on, and as soon as he accessed the label technology, he and Le Mauvais set the whole elaborate scheme in motion.

Hardware readily admitted to inserting the thumb drive to sabotage the tracking system to recruiting and paying Moonbeam for her role. It started with a call he made to her when he posed as a top executive at GeoFibre and talked her into sharing the crucial information about Will's whereabouts. He paid her one hundred thousand dollars in cash and told her to make up a story about where it came from, if anyone asked. While Moonbeam gathered information about Will's progress, Hardware was hard at work in the lab. After getting his hands on one of Will's labels, and under the guise of creating an ordinary GeoFibre tracking device, he programmed this one so it would track only Will's things in particular.

But his job was more elaborate. Once he completed work on the scanning device and safely left it at the drop spot Lana Lang had requested, he was back in the lab. It was a tricky job to code a virus strong enough to incapacitate the tracking database, and due to time constraints, he cut corners. The virus wasn't able to wipe out GeoFibre's data permanently, and he had to settle for a temporary block. It was that shortcut that allowed the GeoFibre team to get their systems back up faster than he imagined. It saved Will and cost Hardware in the end. He said Le Mauvais wanted to meet him personally, which was how Streaming and Will saw them together on the trail.

Fortunately for Alain, he closed off the trail before they

could leave the area, and that night at The White Horse they had genuinely surprised each other when they both showed up at the same dinner. Since their new situation forced them into the public eye and they had not prepared how to coordinate their stories, they used visual cues and kicks to the feet under the table. Hardware told the authorities that Le Mauvais never completely trusted him. She heard about his prowess in the bedroom and was fearful he would spill crucial information to Moonbeam in the heat of passion.

"It was a total coincidence that neither Lana Lang nor Hardware had any idea that Moonbeam was Esther Blankenship, the woman he'd been paying off for our company secrets," said Alain. They didn't find out until they all met at The White Horse."

"I knew we'd uncover plenty of information with them all together. I only wish I'd picked up on that tidbit earlier," said Alain.

"Speaking of tidbits, I've got one you won't believe. The autopsy showed that she didn't undergo a complete transition. From the waist down, Lana Lang was still all man."

Alain poured himself another drink. "I have to hand it to her for only doing the minimum to make herself unrecognizable. She wanted get back in the game as fast as possible."

Gear Junkie asked for an update on Growler. Alain hoped to bring him into custody alive, but Mother Nature had other plans. After Becky handcuffed him and turned him over to a local police officer for safekeeping at the Maryland side of the bridge, she got called back urgently to the bridge. Between that time and Lana Lang's jump, Growler overpowered the cop and got away. While his escape was an inconvenience, it was not a concern, and they chalked it off as a delay.

"He was good at lifting credit cards and stealing cars, but he was so unskilled at hiking and camping Becky knew it wouldn't take long to find him again, and it turned out to be easier than they thought, thanks to Moonbeam."

"Moonbeam?"

"Yes, she ran into him the next day on the trail," said Alain.

"What was she doing up there? Last thing I remember, she was distraught over Hardware's arrest."

"Never underestimate the resilience of that woman," added Alain. "She met another guy in a bar that same night, and apparently by noon the next day she had him on the trail with her. A little over an hour into their hike, they stumbled upon him, or at least his body. During the night, one or more bears savagely tore him apart."

Gear Junkie was astonished. "So, those stories really were true?"

Alain smiled. "Yes and no. What was true was that bears wanted his food, like the poster said. And no wonder, because this time he had a lot of food on him. It was just that to eat it, they had to get him first. Apparently, they have a taste for veggie burgers, too. Remember how he stuffed his pockets with them?"

Suzen was still confused. "With all their elaborate planning, I would have thought Hardware or Lana Lang would have known what you looked like, Alain. If she was so eager to get revenge on you, why wasn't she able to recognize you?"

"It's that context thing again," said Will. "Never in a million years would she expect to find him on a farm in wild and wonderful West Virginia."

"Well, I found it hard to believe nobody picked up on your name," said Suzen. "I thought picking Tracker was risky."

"Speaking of names, you know, after all this, I'm not sure what to call you," said Gear Junkie. "You have so many names. Which one should I use? Tracker? Red Rover? Or maybe one of your real ones?"

Will laughed and pulled out his standby answer. "Take your pick. I answer to any of them."

"Yeah, I guess we all came out of this with extra identities. I wish you could have heard me playing Frank's controlling wife on the other end of the phone," said Suzen. "I have to admit that was fun."

"By the way, even though we all know your real name now, I'm afraid it's too late for me to change. You will always be Gear Junkie to me," joked Will.

After dinner, Gear Junkie excused himself to catch a train. When only the three of them remained, Will made a confession.

"I still feel awful about Patrick Myers. If I hadn't fallen asleep, he might still be alive."

Alain patted him on the shoulder. "There is nothing you could have done. Le Mauvais was a real pro. Under the circumstances, you and I were both lucky to get out of this unharmed."

"I thought Major M's men were trailing everyone that night. I don't understand how she made it to Jefferson Rock and killed Streaming without my hearing her."

Alain sighed. "It's regrettable, but we underestimated her. They watched her check in at the hostel, but she slipped out again somehow. Maybe she was wearing a disguise."

Will made another confession. "You know, reliving this adventure has made something clear. Honestly, I don't know if I can go back to work at the Foundation."

"Hey listen, I understand," said Suzen. "I can handle things for a while. Take all the time you need."

"No, that's not what I mean. I'm fine, but this was such a rush." He paused. "I'm afraid I'd be bored."

"I know what you mean," said Alain. "It's got its thrills, but as you've learned, my line of work can be dangerous."

"Yeah, but it turns out hiking can be dangerous, too."

"Touché!" laughed Alain.

"I have to agree with Will on this one," Suzen said. "My job seems a little dull, too."

Alain retrieved a bottle of Champagne. "I may have a solution," he said, pouring it into crystal flutes. "Remember that Cipher project Will heard Hardware talking about? I mentioned the name to Major M, and it rang a bell. He asked if I was interested in getting involved. When I suggested the Foundation might make the perfect cover for our involvement, he agreed."

"What do you mean 'our involvement?'" Will asked.

Alain shrugged. "I may be the brains behind the operation, but I need to retire from the physical part. Losing Le Mauvais on the bridge taught me that the hard way. I was thinking you could be my man on the ground."

Will's eyes bulged. "Seriously? Do you think I'm ready?"

"I don't know. Why not? I've been training you all your life. What do you think learning all those languages and taking those acting classes were for? Besides, it sounds like Suzen wants in, too."

Suzen raised her glass. "I'm up for it, if you are."

Will hemmed. "I don't know. It depends. Do I get to keep my teeth this time?"

THE END

ABOUT THE AUTHOR

Following an exciting life-long career in advertising, Alan B. Gibson cofounded a video-chat technology startup that often competes for time with his novel writing.

FOLLOW A. B. GIBSON

If you liked *Tracked to Kill*, please do me the favor of leaving a review on a site that reviews books. To learn about me and my other books, visit www.ABGibson.me. You can also follow me on Facebook, Twitter, and Instagram.

Other books in The Appalachian Trail Murder Mysteries series

The Dead of Winter

Four young professionals pick the wrong weekend to overnight at a family friendly pumpkin patch bed and breakfast. It's the last day of the season, and the weather and the farm are picture perfect. Ma and Pa Winter are the consummate hosts, and they immediately win over Dillon, Tara, Josh, and Julia with their homespun authenticity.

Like the thousands of other visitors to Winters Farm and Orchard, the four are eager to pick apples and pumpkins and take the challenge of the Giant Corn Maze, but Ma Winter has other plans. A scary moonlight hayride spirals into a frantic twenty-four hours of deception and mayhem, and the group finds themselves unwilling participants in a horrific family tradition.

High Voltage

He had a couple of weeks to kill. When Strider, an unassuming hiker fresh off the Appalachian Trail, needs extra cash, a curio shop owner suggests Winter's Farm, a popular stop for hikers looking for day work. What seems like a lucky break turns into a series of horrors as one by one his fellow hikers disappear, including his fiancée. A cast of colorful characters complicates his quest to find her, and after stumbling upon the dark truth, his search turns to a desperate escape from the farm's kooky owner. But a foreboding electric fence stymies his chance of freedom in *High Voltage*, A. B. Gibson's most thrilling novel yet.